D0564239

"First of all, as I said, I'm from almost eighty years in your future. How old do you think I am?"

"About sixty," he answered honestly.

"Thanks," the old man replied, grinning. "I'm actually ninety-two."

"Ninety-two?" Brandon stared at him in amazement. "Then you're very well preserved."

The man shrugged. "In eighty years, there have been a lot of medical advances," he replied. "So I'm in actually quite good form. It's possible I'll live for another fifty or sixty years yet."

"Cool," Brandon replied. "But what's this got to do with me?"

"It's got everything to do with you, Brandon," the time traveler answered. "You see, I'm not just *any* ninety-two-year-old man from eighty years in the future. I'm *you*. I'm Brandon Mooney."

NORTH DEARBORN LIBRARY

The Outer Limits™

A whole new dimension in
adventure . . .

*forthcoming from Tor Kids!

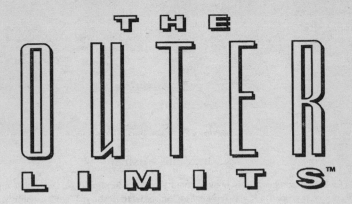

THE OUTER LIMITS™

THE TIME SHIFTER

JOHN PEEL

Tor Kids!

A TOM DOHERTY ASSOCIATES BOOK
NEW YORK

NOTE: If you purchased this book without a cover you should be aware that this book is stolen property. It was reported as "unsold and destroyed" to the publisher, and neither the author nor the publisher has received any payment for this "stripped book."

This is a work of fiction. All the characters and events portrayed in this book are either products of the author's imagination or are used fictitiously.

THE OUTER LIMITS # 3: THE TIME SHIFTER

Copyright © 1997 Outer Productions Inc. All rights reserved.
The Outer Limits is a trademark of Metro-Goldwyn-Mayer Inc, and is licensed by MGM Consumer Products.

Cover art by Peter Bollinger

A Tor Book
Published by Tom Doherty Associates, Inc.
175 Fifth Avenue
New York, NY 10010

TOR® is a registered trademark of Tom Doherty Associates, Inc.

ISBN: 0-812-59065-1

First edition: November 1997

Printed in the United States of America

0 9 8 7 6 5 4 3 2 1

For Tom Beck

Throughout human history, people have wondered what it would be like to have the power to travel in time. What would happen if you could return to the past and change some action that has happened to you? Would you be able to set right something that once went wrong? Or would your actions, however well intentioned, create worse troubles than those you began with? Would you have the wisdom to know what should be changed and what should be left unaltered?

Of course, nobody has such a power.

Nobody in our time, that is.

Unless they had returned here from some future date . . .

CHAPTER 1

IT WAS ALMOST time. The assassin could sense that. There was a stirring within him as he crouched across the branch of the tree, peering into the window opposite him, his rifle cradled gently but firmly in his left hand. He glanced at his chrono, and saw that it was slightly past ten P.M. And Henry Brandt ran almost fanatically on time.

The assassin had been waiting patiently for him for more than an hour. It wasn't wasted time. Brandt's estate was large and extremely well guarded. For the turn of the century, that was. There was a tall wire fence surrounding the entire eight-acre site, far too high for a man to jump. And if anyone tried to climb it, they would almost certainly be spotted by one of the armed guards, or by one of the highly trained mastiffs. And if the men and the dogs somehow missed seeing such an intruder, then the motion detectors embedded in the fence would surely sound an alarm.

And if the intruder did somehow still make it across the fence, the yard, too, was wired with motion detectors, heat sensors and undoubtedly lots of other high-tech gadgets that were absolutely guaranteed to find a grasshopper munching on a leaf.

And none of them had stood the slightest chance of detecting the assassin whatsoever.

The problem was that they were looking at him in entirely the wrong way. He eased open his slightly cramped fingers again, and smiled to himself. Brandt's neighbors thought the industrialist was paranoid, and that his security measures were far too strict. They especially thought this when a low-flying owl set off the sensors and sounded the alarms from time to time. Their complaints to Brandt were met by complete indifference. Brandt felt secure, wrapped up in his technological cocoon, certain that nothing short of a small army could get at him once he was in his home. He'd taken the old expression about a man's home being his castle to the logical conclusion: he'd made his house as impregnable as modern technology could offer.

A castle, he thought. A prison, to others.

Unfortunately, this time Henry Brandt was up against more than modern technology.

For the assassin to bypass all the security devices had been simplicity itself—if you happened to own a personal time-field generator, which the assassin did. It was woven into the fabric of the black coverall that he was wearing, with the simple controls on his belt. If he had tried to get into Brandt's fortress in this time, he'd have been caught for certain.

So he hadn't tried that at all. He'd simply set his controls for twenty years in the past, before Brandt had built his beautiful home. He had then strolled through the thick copse of trees until he came to the one that would overlook the study window of Henry Brandt in twenty years' time. He had climbed the tree, and unslung the rifle from his shoulder. Then he had settled down comfortably and projected himself twenty years back into the future, in the same spot in the same tree.

And now, here he was, watching the study window opposite him, and waiting for the punctual Mr. Brandt to reach his study at 10:05, as he did every single night of his life.

Only this would be the very last time he would perform this ritual.

Brandt was one of the most powerful men in America, though few people outside of his immediate circle realized this. In an age when millionaires seemed to be as common as flies, and billionaires barely worth mentioning, Brandt was one of the wealthiest men in the country. Yet his name never appeared in the columns of *Fortune* magazine, or on the list of the richest men in the world, even though he was probably number three on such a list. Because Brandt hated personal publicity. He was a very private person who loathed having to share anything about himself with anyone else. It made him feel insecure for anyone to really know anything about him.

So he had contrived to stay hidden from public view. He had accumulated his money and his influence through various companies and industries of which he owned the bulk—very quietly. He never gave interviews, and rarely met the thousands of people who worked for him. He had two private secretaries with whom he would meet and speak once a day.

He had an accountant and a lawyer. And no one else in the world of business at all.

He did have a wife, of course. Brandt knew that he would not be able to live forever, and he had no intention of letting his empire or fortune collapse when he died. He had found himself a beautiful wife, and they had had a single child, a son, who was now seventeen. He would be the heir to the Brandt fortune when Brandt died.

In about five minutes, in fact.

Mrs. Brandt was very obliging towards her husband's idiosyncrasies. She didn't find her husband's wish to be left strictly alone a bother at all. It turned out that the beautiful Mrs. Brandt was as warm as an iceberg. Her only real love was her husband's money, and he gave her whatever of that she wished. No matter how extravagant her tastes, she could barely make a dent in his funds. So both had what they wanted out of their relationship: she the money, the social whirl, and the expensive and exotic vacations; he a son and heir, and otherwise peace and solitude.

The assassin found all of this vastly amusing. True, Brandt's plan had worked very well—while he was alive. But almost from the second he had died in 2027, word about his power had leaped out into the world, which was stunned to discover just how much influence he had. And since the assassin came from a time more than fifty years beyond 2027, he knew everything about Henry Brandt. None of his secrets were safe.

Nor was his life, despite all of these precautions.

Very nearly time now. The assassin readied the rifle, looking directly ahead through the thick leaves toward the study window. Brandt was a creature of terrible habit. He liked his life to be absolutely just *so*, and no other way. He had his meals precisely on time; he met his contacts at rigidly prescribed hours, and he checked his stocks and investments at the same moment every business day. And at 10:05 every evening, he entered his private study, where the butler would pour him a large vermouth and then leave. Brandt always took thirty-two minutes to consume the drink, and then would retire alone to his bed.

But tonight that precise regimen would end.

10:05.

The door to the study opened, and Henry Brandt marched in. There was strict discipline in every line of his body. His graying hair was swept back from his high forehead. His suit, shirt and tie were impeccable. He looked utterly unflappable and totally in command of every situation. The butler followed him in, poured the drink, bowed and left the room.

Brandt was alone, sipping at the glass and thinking whatever business thoughts might be passing through his mind. He was undoubtedly not thinking about dying within the next two minutes. Perhaps he was thinking about the upcoming legislation he was sponsoring. Confidentially, of course. The new proposal had become very controversial, pitting polluters versus environmentalists. Profits versus trees. A very severe law had been passed the year before that had drastically reduced certain pollutants in factories. It had also, however, cut deep into the profits of Henry Brandt. He had bought a congressman or two and a senator or three, and he was just starting his efforts to weaken the laws that were limiting the growth and profits of his company.

And he would succeed, too, in a year or so. The teeth of the current law would be yanked out, and Brandt's companies would be able to make their extra profits. They would also increase the pollution in America's rivers, poison wildlife and fish and ultimately cause the toxic waste that would kill almost a million people in 2043.

Brandt didn't realize that this was what his greed would lead to. He sincerely believed that it was better for the country that his industries should employ more people and make more goods. And that liberals trying to save endangered frogs were being impractical and overly cautious. None of which made the slightest bit of difference, of course. His actions would still kill almost a million people, and they would impoverish the United States for more than a generation. Eighty-seven endangered species of birds, animals, and fish would perish because of the loosened laws. And the world in the assassin's home time would be impoverished and unpleasant to live in.

At least, until now it had been. But the assassin was about to alter all that.

He brought the rifle into position, aiming carefully. He could see Brandt clearly in the electronic sights. If it were pitch black, he would be able to see him absolutely clearly. He focused in on Brandt's heart, and steadied his nerves.

Brandt would be his sixth victim. But his conscience still gave him trouble when he tried to pull the trigger. Did Henry Brandt really deserve to die? he wondered.

Yes, he answered himself. Henry Brandt was a very dangerous man. Not an evil man, say, like a Hitler. Merely greedy and misguided. But what of *his* millions of victims? And the eighty-seven now-extinct species of animal life? Did *they* deserve to die? His serenity of purpose returned slowly. He realized he was doing the right thing. After all, what was the life of one man against the life of a million?

His finger tightened on the trigger, and the rifle spat. An electrical pulse passed through the glass without harming it. It was only on contact with living flesh—human or animal—that it discharged its tremendous power.

Brandt clutched at his heart. He probably gasped, but the assassin couldn't hear that through the glass. The drink fell from his paralyzed fingers, and then Brandt followed it to the floor. There was no need to check; he was dead.

The murder would be completely undetectable. When Brandt's body was found in the morning, it would look as if he'd simply had a heart attack and died. There would be no trace of a weapon. Of course, even if there *were* suspicions, the police search for an intruder would be fruitless. After all, with the fence and the guards and the dogs and the motion detectors, it would have been impossible for anyone to break in. Especially without leaving the slightest trace.

The assassin smiled. With Brandt dead, the future was safe. The new law relaxing pollution standards would not pass. The eighty-seven species of wildlife would not die. A million people would survive.

The assassin calmly triggered his personal time-field generator, and slipped back twenty years again. Then he clambered down out of the tree, and walked back through the woods to where he had left his other equipment. Once there, he replaced the bolt rifle in its case, and opened another case. This one contained nothing but his Helmet.

His hands were shaking slightly as he prepared to don the Helmet. It was spherical, with no way of seeing the outside world once it was fitted snugly over his head. But he didn't need to see anything outside when he had the Helmet on. Inside, it would project a perfectly real-seeming three-dimensional picture into his optical nerves. It was connected to a machine he had left in his laboratory in the future.

It would show him what the world of his home time now was like, with Brandt dead more than twenty years before he was supposed to have died. It would show a better world than the one he had known. He would have set right what once had gone terribly wrong.

He pulled the Helmet over his head, cutting off the woods from his view. The act of donning the Helmet triggered its program. He saw darkness for only a brief second, and then the world about him lit up.

It appeared as if he were actually standing on the balcony of his laboratory, looking toward the hillside beyond. In his time, the hillside had been denuded of almost all life. The soil had been far too poisoned to allow grass or plants to grow. No animals ranged on its hills, no birds nested in its trees, no insects drifted across bubbling streams. The stream at the base of the hill had been a faint brown color, and when the wind was blowing in the right direction, you could smell the decay.

"Oh my—" He wasn't prepared for what he saw.

The hill was now utterly devoid of life. Scraped clean. The river was a sluggish red liquid that twisted like a rusty wound through the earth. There was no sound of any kind of life at all.

Pain and anger lanced through him. The assassin tore off the Helmet, tempted to throw it against the ground in frustration and agony. But his better sense prevented him from damaging his precious link to his own era.

He'd changed the future by killing Brandt, all right—for the worse.

He had failed . . . again.

CHAPTER 2

BRANDON MOONEY REALIZED his life—already in the pits—had just taken a steep drop downward. He stared down at Rory Tucker in dismay. The other boy was on his back on the floor, his books scattered, his note still falling like an autumn leaf. Colliding with Rory had hurt Brandon, but not as much as he knew it was going to.

He tried to salvage what he could of the situation, just in case Rory was in an uncharacteristically good mood. "Gee, I'm *sorry*, Rory," he apologized. "That was really clumsy of me. Let me help you." He stretched out a hand to the other boy, but Rory batted it away, his face flushed.

"You just made a fatal mistake, then," he growled, levering himself to his feet. "Nobody tries to push me around and gets away with it."

Brandon's stomach did a backflip. "I wasn't trying to push

you around, honest," he said. "I was just in a rush, and—"

"Save it," said Rory. "You're going to pay in blood, and that's it."

Brandon was five eight, but very skinny. Rory was six feet, and built like a brick wall. He had about the same IQ as a wall, too. Once he had an idea in his mind, it was difficult to dislodge, since there weren't very many others to replace it with. And he'd enjoyed picking on Brandon in the past. Now he was justifying beating Brandon up. And Brandon knew he didn't stand a chance of fighting off Rory.

It was definitely time to hit the road and hope he could run faster than Rory. Since the other boy was on the football team and Brandon's usual exercise was moving his mouse around its pad, he doubted he could. But running had to offer a better chance than standing still and waiting for the bully to beat him to a pulp.

But Rory's friends and the rest of the students had figured out what Brandon was going to do. They'd formed a circle around him and Rory. It looked fairly loose, but Brandon understood that if he tried to make a dash for it, the circle would solidify and trap him.

He was doomed.

Rory bunched his fists, a faint smile on his face, as he moved in for the kill. Brandon knew he didn't stand a chance, and he tried one last appeal.

"Come on, Rory," he begged. "It was an accident. And I'm not worth your time, really I'm not."

"I've got nothing better to do," Rory snarled, and his fist lashed out, pretty lightly, all things considered.

Brandon froze like a startled deer in the headlights of a roaring sixteen-wheeler. He didn't have a clue how he was supposed to block it. He'd never been a very physical person. The punch landed on his forearm, and hurt. He gave a yelp and jumped back. Several of the boys watching snickered at this.

"Come on, rabbit," one called. "That wasn't even a *punch.*"

"Yeah," said Brianne Waite, rolling her eyes. "Get a grip."

"Rory, please," Brandon begged, knowing it was futile.

"Come on, chicken," Rory taunted, jabbing at him again. "At least *pretend* to defend yourself. Don't make this too easy for me." He punched Brandon in the stomach, still not too hard. Brandon recognized the strategy. The punch was only meant to taunt him, to soften him up, to lull him into thinking that he might actually have a chance against Rory. And then Rory would pulverize him.

Trying to fight back would do no good at all. Brandon moved back, warily watching Rory's fists. Hands behind him pushed him forward again, jeering him on. Brandon stumbled, and studied Rory desperately. "I'm not going to fight you," he gasped. "And you don't need to fight me."

"What a total geek," Rory complained. He punched Brandon again, harder, and Brandon yelped. "Take your medicine like a man," Rory told him. "Don't squawk like a chicken." His fist lashed out again, hitting Brandon's right bicep painfully.

Brandon knew he was doomed, and he continued futilely to try to get out of Rory's way. He held his hands out, not exactly blocking the blows, but in a weak protest. Rory gave a growl of disgust, and then punched higher.

There was a blur across Brandon's vision, and then a smack

of pure pain in his nose. There was a sticky sensation, and the sharp tang of fresh blood. Brandon gave a groan, and felt blood flowing down his face. Rory had given him a bloody nose. Panic set in firmly now. Rory had drawn blood, and Brandon expected the sight and smell of it to excite him like any other dumb animal, and that he would go for the kill.

Instead, there was a girl's voice: "Rory Tucker, stop that immediately! Let him alone!"

Brandon winced as he saw Toni Frost shove a couple of taller boys out of her way and force herself into the circle. She looked furious, and pushed between him and Rory.

"What do you think you're doing?" she snapped at him angrily.

Rory looked sullen, but let his fists drop to his side. There was a smudge of Brandon's blood on the right knuckles. "Teaching him a lesson."

"You?" Toni snorted. "You can't even *spell* lesson, let alone teach one. You're just being a bully, as usual. Leave him alone."

"Why should I?" Rory demanded.

"Because if you don't, I'm fetching the principal," Toni snapped. "And I don't think you need another detention, do you?" She stared him down, and Rory turned away.

"Ah, he's a chicken anyway," he complained. "I won't soil my hands with him."

"That has to be the first smart thing you've done all day," Toni told him as he stooped to pick up his books and papers. Realizing that there wasn't going to be any murder, the other students started to drift away.

Toni whirled around on Brandon next. "And whatever possessed you to pick a fight with that bully?" she demanded, pulling a wad of tissues from her backpack and handing them to him. "I thought you had more sense than that."

Accepting the tissues, Brandon held them under his nose, trying to stop the stinging flow. "I bumped into him by accident," he explained. He was furiously embarrassed. Being attacked by Rory had been bad enough, but being saved by a girl was even more humiliating. He almost would have preferred being pounded senseless. The thing was that Toni was a Good Samaritan, always looking for causes to throw herself into. Saving the whales, adopting stray dogs and cats, hugging trees—anything she could give her heart to was fine with her. And it looked like she'd made him her project for the day.

"Accidents like that can get you killed," she replied, examining him critically. "Come on, we'd better get you to the nurse so she can take a look at that nose."

"I don't need your help," he snapped ungraciously.

Toni snorted again. "Right. You had Rory exactly where you wanted him, didn't you? Brandon, you are a world-class doofus, you know that?"

"And you're an interfering girl," he snapped back, and immediately wished he could have thought of something a little more intelligent and cutting. He never could until he replayed the events later in his mind, over and over, and invented all kinds of snappy comebacks that simply never occurred to him at the time.

"Well, I'm glad to see that you've managed to identify my sex correctly, at least," she answered. "Come on."

Following her would cause the least number of problems, so Brandon did so. He was burning with embarrassment. He'd been beaten up—okay, maybe only mildly, but it had been very effective—in front of most of the guys in his class. And he'd been saved from worse only because Toni had sailed in to rescue him. How much worse could his life get?

"You need a keeper," she informed him.

"Are you volunteering for the job?" he growled, not really thinking about what he was saying. To his surprise, she turned around and looked him over critically.

"You're a ninety-six-pound weakling," she decided. "Without the courage to fight back."

"Fighting's barbaric," he answered weakly.

Toni grinned. "True. But we live in a barbaric society. You can't escape it by being a pacifist, Brandon, no matter how much you believe in the cause."

"I don't believe in pacifism!" he snapped back. "But if I'd tried to fight back, Rory would have done a lot worse to me than bloody my nose."

"You're right about that," she agreed. "So, as I said, you need a keeper. Maybe I should stick around you for the next few days."

That made Brandon blush even more. Being seen around school in the company of a girl would wreck whatever tattered reputation he might have left at this point. Of course, if it was a total babe like Brianne Waite, it could be accepted, envied, even. Brianne was a to-die-for blond bombshell, and every guy in school drooled around her. Naturally, she loathed Brandon, and he'd felt the cut of her barbed words more than once. Like during the fight . . .

Toni wasn't exactly a toad, though. She had short-cropped dark hair, and a fairly nice face. But she wasn't acceptable hanging-out material for any of the guys in school. Not that this seemed to matter to her at all. She was friendly enough with the other girls, but had a tendency to hang out by herself.

She was forthright, opinionated and in your face.

Just the kind of person Brandon couldn't stand to be around.

"Thanks, but I'll pass on your kind offer," he told her.

"It's not your decision," she replied. "Come on, the nurse is waiting. So, why did Rory pick on you, anyway?"

"Why does rain fall downward?" Brandon replied. "It just does. Rory picks on people who are smarter than him—which is pretty much the rest of the human race. If you consider him human. It makes him mad when he realizes he's as dumb as an ox, and he hates me because I'm way better than him."

"You've got a high opinion of yourself, haven't you?" Toni asked.

"And why shouldn't I?" he retorted. "I'm the brightest kid in this school, and everyone knows it."

Toni stared hard at him again, and he had to look away. "If you were less conceited and showed off less, people wouldn't dislike you as much as they do," she informed him.

"I don't care what people think about me," he growled. "They're not worth considering."

"And arrogant, too," Toni said, as if to herself. "What a wonderful combination! Arrogance, anger, conceit and cowardice." She shook her head. "Definitely not prime material."

"Then leave me alone," Brandon demanded, annoyed by her criticism. "I didn't ask for your help—or your company."

She simply ignored his protests, pushing open the door to the nurse's office. As he brushed past her to enter, she barred his way with her arm. "I'm going to watch over you, whether you like it or not. So why not make it a pleasant experience? How about sodas and pizza after school? Your treat?"

"No way," he replied. "I am not being seen around with you."

She laughed. "Guess again," she informed him. "See you later." And she breezed off, leaving him standing in the doorway.

What did she think she was doing? There was no way that Brandon was going to hang out with her. For one thing, he didn't want her around. For another, he'd get picked on even more. For another—

He gave up in disgust, and went in to get his nose seen to.

This day was the pits. Brandon had managed to avoid Toni after the nurse had fixed him up, but he knew his good luck wouldn't last. Why was she doing this to him? Was he another of her strays that she'd decided to adopt? Or did she fancy him, for some strange reason? Well, either way, he'd figure out some way to put her off.

Then he saw her coming down the corridor, straight toward him. Brandon panicked, and looked around for somewhere to escape to.

The boy's room! With a smile of triumph, he ducked inside. Even Toni Frost wouldn't follow him in here. He was safe for a while, at least. He dropped his backpack to the floor, and wandered over to the sinks. He studied his reflection in the mirror. His nose was slightly swollen and very red still, but otherwise, he didn't look too bad. He could feel a tender area on his arm, under his shirt, and knew he had a bruise there. All in all, though, he'd gotten out of the fight with surprisingly little damage. The only problem was that he owed Toni for the rescue, and that hurt more than his nose or arm.

Why wouldn't she just leave him alone?

He stared in the mirror again, and then splashed a little water on his face. It helped to cool him off a little.

Then he stiffened. Something odd was happening in the mirror. It was clouding slightly, as if steam were blurring it up. But there was no steam. Brandon was puzzled, but he figured that it was just another thing going wrong with the school. It was over forty years old, and all sorts of leaks and other malfunctions were continually happening. A mirror clouding over was nothing to worry about.

He could see that his image was blurring, the focus shifting. And then Brandon realized something very odd indeed. He stared at the mirror in shock. Though his image was blurred and shifting, the background in the mirror was still perfectly in focus.

It was just the portion of the mirror that reflected his image that was changing . . .

And it *was* changing. His reflection had somehow grown a couple of inches taller, and fleshed out a little. And then it snapped back instantly into focus.

Only it wasn't his face staring back out at him. It was the face of an older man, someone maybe in his sixties. It looked a little bit like him, but it was obviously someone else entirely. He stared at it in shock. What was happening here? How could this be? A mirror was supposed to show you yourself, not some old guy!

And then the reflection said, "Hello, Brandon."

CHAPTER 3

BRANDON WONDERED IF Rory might not have hit him harder in the head than he'd first thought. He *had* to be hallucinating! A reflection that wasn't his own, talking to him through a mirror . . . he *knew* that this was neither possible nor normal.

The reflection, however, didn't seem to know that. "Relax," it advised him. "I'm not imaginary, and you're not crazy. This is an emergency, and there wasn't any other way to contact you."

Shaking his head in disbelief, Brandon backed slowly away from the mirror. The image, however, stayed where it was. Brandon swallowed, fighting down panic. He must be going crazy to see and hear things, but there was no way he was going crazy enough to attempt to answer a hallucination back.

"I knew that this would be difficult for you," the old man

said. "And it's going to get harder, too. But I have to see you, and in a lot more solid form than this." He gestured at himself and sighed. "Stand back a bit further."

That was something that Brandon needed no urging to do. He was about ready to flee the rest room, in fact. The only thing that held him back right now was his fear that the hallucination might go with him, and then everyone in the school might see him going crazy. If he was going to lose his mind, he preferred not to have witnesses. So he backed up to the far wall.

"Right," said the old man. His hand disappeared from the mirror, as if he was adjusting some sort of equipment. "Here I come."

And then the mirror seemed to ripple, like water when a stone is dropped into it. Only in this case, the stone was coming out. Or, rather, the man was. Somehow, he was stepping out of the mirror, as if it were a doorway to some other place. He balanced on the edge of the sink for a moment, but as it creaked under the strain, he jumped down to the floor, pretty nimbly for a person his apparent age.

He was dressed in some kind of dark costume, a one-piece jumpsuit like Air Force pilots wore. He had on boots the same color. There was a wide belt at his waist, with several small controls and lights that flickered oddly. He looked rather amused, and glanced around the room with a faint air of disgust.

"I'd forgotten how squalid these places were," he commented. Then he crossed to where Brandon was staring at him in astonishment and held out a hand. "Nice to finally meet you, Brandon," he said.

Automatically, Brandon accepted the grip and shook a very

real hand. If this man was an illusion, then this was as real as anything Brandon had ever known. At least if he was going crazy, he was doing it with style! "Who are you?" he demanded. "And how did you do that?"

"Well, at least you're talking," the man answered. "I'd rather not answer the first question just now, because the answer will get complicated. As for the second . . ." He chewed at his lip for a minute. "It's a matter of generating fields of potential. Kind of like virtual reality, if you like, only with the potential of moving from virtual to real reality. It's rather too advanced a concept for you to understand yet, but you'll comprehend the whole thing very well in about thirty years. In fact, you'll invent it."

"Invent it?" This wasn't making any sense to Brandon at all. How could this man know what Brandon would do with his life? Nobody could, since Brandon didn't believe in all that psychic trash that ended up in supermarket tabloids and best-selling books. Except . . . There was another possibility. "Are you from the future?"

The man grinned. "You've got it on the first try," he said happily. "I am indeed. From about eighty years in the future, in fact. And I have to talk to you and show you some things, because I need your help."

"Go ahead," Brandon said. He was rather surprised at how quickly he'd accepted that the man was telling the truth. It was the only possibility that made sense if Brandon wasn't going insane. And he didn't believe that he was. Of course, if he *was* going crazy, naturally he wouldn't think he was. Still, he *had* to believe he was OK unless there was ever any proof otherwise.

"Not now," the man said. "And certainly not here. Anyone could walk in at any time. Meet me after school in the woods. You know where.''

"Huh?'' Brandon stared at him in confusion. "How can I know where when I don't know who you are?''

"Your private spot,'' the man replied. "Trust me, I know it as well as you do. And the fact that I do should help prove my story when we meet again. Right now, I'd better leave before anyone else runs into me. I'll see you later, Brandon.'' He gave a quick salute, then touched the controls on his belt. The mirror started to shimmer again, and the man leaped lightly onto the sink and then plunged back into the mirror. It whirled again, and then Brandon was staring only at his own reflection once more.

He leaned forward, feeling weak at the knees. This was simply so wild that it was almost unbelievable. A man claiming to be from the future wanted to meet him after school. . . . It seemed so crazy, but Brandon had to assume it wasn't. It was shocking, yes, and disturbing; but it couldn't be crazy. He splashed water on his face again, and dried off. Then he left the bathroom.

Only to wince when he saw Toni Frost staring at him. He'd forgotten about her!

"You took long enough,'' she said.

"Not long enough,'' Brandon replied with a groan. "You're still here. Why don't you leave me in peace? I don't want you around.''

"We're going for pizza after school, remember?'' she informed him.

"I never agreed to that!'' he protested. "Look, I don't know why you've suddenly become interested in me, and I don't care. Just leave me alone, OK?''

"And let you get yourself beaten up again?" Toni asked sweetly.

"If I want to be, yes." Brandon didn't want to play word games with her. "It's my life, and I'll do with it whatever I please. Not whatever you or anyone else pleases."

She gave him an odd look. "You're very self-confident, aren't you?" she demanded.

"Yes," Brandon replied. "And I've a right to be. I'm the smartest kid in school, and the smartest kid this school has ever seen—or will see. I may not be much for the physical side of things, but my brain's better than any ten other people's put together."

"And modest, too," she added dryly. "Even if you *are* as smart as you claim, telling people that sort of thing might put them off."

"Like you?" he suggested rudely.

Toni shook her head. "No. Nothing much puts me off once I've made up my mind. You may be the smartest kid in school, but I'll bet I'm the most stubborn."

Brandon gave a sigh. "And the most irritating."

"True." Nothing seemed to be capable of insulting her. "So, I'll see you after school, then?"

"No," he growled. "For one thing, I don't want to be seen with you. For another, I've got something to do. So leave me alone." He turned and stomped off down the corridor.

"Tomorrow, then," she called after him. "I can be patient. But not for long."

Brandon's face was burning. Why was she doing this to him? Why couldn't she just leave him alone? He didn't want her company; why couldn't she understand that?

He drew up short as he realized that he'd almost bumped

into someone else. He had to stop letting his mind roam and focus on getting through the school safely. He looked at the person he'd almost plowed into: Brianne. "Uh, hi," he muttered, burning red.

Brianne raised an eyebrow, and gave him a disgusted look. "Well, if it isn't the human chicken," she sneered. "Trying to knock me down, too? If you do, chicken boy, I'll do more than bloody your nose for you, and that's a promise."

Not knowing what to say, Brandon stood there feeling really stupid and embarrassed. With a snort of irritation, Brianne shoved past him and stormed off down the corridor.

Brandon abruptly realized that this exchange had been witnessed when one of his classmates jeered, "Way to go, Romeo!" There was laughter from the dozen or so kids watching him. Blushing even worse, Brandon hurried away. Couldn't he do *anything* right?

They were all picking on him. It wasn't his fault, he knew. They were all intimidated and jealous of him because he was so much smarter than they were. They just used any excuse they could to make him look bad. It was a classic compensation tactic: to make yourself look good, make people who are better than you look bad. Only it wouldn't work in his case. He *knew* he was better than them; their mockery couldn't really hurt him.

Maybe not. But it sure could sting.

The rest of the day dragged slowly. Several times one or more of the other students would make chicken noises at him, or fold their arms into "wings" and pretend to flutter them. Despite the shame, he tried to ignore them. They were ignorant idiots whose opinions were as worthless as their minds. But being the butt of all the humor everyone else was sharing didn't make him comfortable. Eventually, though, lessons were over, and Brandon fled school.

His parents both worked, so he had no set time to actually be home by. He could do whatever he wanted for the next couple of hours, and he knew what he had to do. He hurried from the school to the nearby woods. It was actually the remnant of an abandoned building project. Several houses had been built about fifteen years earlier, including his own. But the builders had gone bankrupt, and the rest of the site had never been developed. As a result, it had left a fairly sizable woods. Even as a child, Brandon had preferred his own company, and about five years ago, he'd found a really cool spot in the woods where an old tree had once stood. It had fallen down during high winds, creating a sort of cave where its roots had been. This had been Brandon's secret spot to retreat to since he'd found it. It had to be where the old man wanted to meet him.

If the old man was real, and not simply a product of Brandon's imagination. But the handshake had felt real enough. And until he had reason to believe otherwise, Brandon had to accept that the man was real, and somehow a time traveler.

In which case, Brandon felt rather excited. He wanted to know more. Why would a time traveler come looking for him? What was happening, and why did he want Brandon's help? It was quite intriguing, and very thrilling.

As Brandon approached the small cave, he saw that the man was already there and waiting. Beside him stood what looked like an overgrown trunk. It was silver, about four feet tall, six long and four wide. As Brandon hurried up, the man raised a hand in greeting.

"I'm glad you swallowed your disbelief," he said by way of greeting. "It's good to see you again."

Brandon nodded, studying the man again. He did look like he might be from another time. His clothing was odd, but not that odd. On the other hand, that belt looked like finer workmanship than anything Brandon had ever seen. And since he was a techno-junkie, Brandon had seen a lot of sophisticated equipment. "You promised me some explanations," he pointed out.

"So I did," the old man agreed, sitting down on his trunk. "And you have to understand me perfectly, so that you'll understand how important it is for you to help me." He gestured for Brandon to join him, so Brandon sat down. "First of all, as I said, I'm from almost eighty years in your future. How old do you think I am?"

Brandon hated questions like that. People always expected you to flatter them by guessing years younger than they actually were. He never did. "About sixty," he answered honestly.

"Thanks," the old man replied, grinning. "I'm actually ninety-two."

"Ninety-two?" Brandon stared at him in amazement. "Then you're very well preserved."

The man shrugged. "In eighty years, there have been a lot of medical advances," he replied. "So I'm in actually quite good form. It's possible I'll live for another fifty or sixty years yet."

"Cool," Brandon replied. "But what's this got to do with me?"

"It's got everything to do with you, Brandon," the time traveler answered. "You see, I'm not just *any* ninety-two-year-old man from eighty years in the future. I'm *you*. I'm Brandon Mooney."

CHAPTER 4

BRANDON STARED AT the old man in shock. He really didn't want to believe him, that *this* was how he would turn out—old, and gray. But . . . well, there was definitely a resemblance, he couldn't deny that. And to know that he would live for at least another eighty years, and be an inventor at that, wasn't all bad. "Me?" he breathed.

"Yes," the traveler answered. "You. That's how I knew about this cave." He waved his hand around. "I've been coming here a long time, at least in my memory. It doesn't exist when I come from."

Brandon tried to get his emotions into working order again. He was simply being overwhelmed, and he had to recover. "What's it like where—*when* you come from?" he asked. "And how did you do it? And what's going to happen to me?"

The old man laughed. "Be patient, and I'll try to answer those questions to the best of my ability—and the best of yours to understand. You see, a lot of what I'll have to tell you won't make much sense yet, since you haven't invented the necessary mechanisms. In fact, I've only just managed to get the time-field generator working in the past month, so there's no way I can explain it simply. Let's just say that it projects a bubble of time around me. Time normally flows in one direction in our universe—from the past to the future. Everyone is embedded in time. What my invention does, so to speak, is take me out of time, so I can reverse my course or accelerate it as I wish. So I can hop back and forward in time."

"You can go anywhere and to any time you like?" Brandon asked eagerly. This was incredible!

"No," his older self replied. "I can only move in *time*, not space. If I jumped from here, this is where I'd end up. So I have to be careful. If I jumped back, oh, twenty years, this tree would still be standing, and I'd arrive inside the trunk. That would kill me rather effectively. There are exceptions, as when I materialized in the mirror. It's move an issue of dimensional permeability."

"Permea-*what*?"

He smiled. "In time. However, I can jump back in time—or forward to my own time—without any other problems. I don't like going very far, though, because I don't know what the land might be like when I arrive. I've jumped back only to this time so far."

"You don't want to explore the past?" asked Brandon, somewhat disappointed in himself. He decided to refer to his older self as "Mooney," to avoid problems.

"I'd love to," Mooney replied. "Except I don't want to land inside a wall, or a tree. So I have to take it slowly and be absolutely certain that I'm not going to do something like that. And, besides that, I didn't invent the time-field generator for fun. I have a mission to perform, which I'll get to in a minute." He smiled. "You asked what was going to happen to you. Well, I can tell you: you're going to become one of the wealthiest and most powerful men in the world."

Brandon stared at him in astonishment. "You're joking," he gasped.

"No, I'm not. Remember, I've lived those years. And I know how brilliant you are. When you leave college, you're going to go into computer design, and in ten years you'll invent the next generation of computers, based on crystal lattices. That will make you rich, and after that, your computers will become the standard for the whole world. Using them, all kinds of incredible machines can be designed. Mankind will begin to really conquer space. And, eventually, you'll be able to invent the time-field generator."

"It sounds pretty awesome," Brandon answered, proud of his achievements. "I can hardly wait to get to work."

Mooney laughed. "That's the spirit. And there are plenty of other rewards for you, too. Remember how all the kids at school used to torment and tease you?"

Brandon nodded. "How could I forget? My nose is still sore from the punch Rory Tucker gave me today."

"Rory Tucker?" Mooney thought for a moment. "Oh, yes, I remember him. Big, stupid bully." He nodded. "In fifteen years, he's going to be a washed-up football player whose investments go sour. He'll shoot himself to death shortly afterward. Serves him right."

Brandon felt odd hearing this. He liked the idea of Rory turning out to be a loser; it didn't surprise him at all, and it seemed to be perfectly appropriate. But the rest of it . . . "Kills himself?"

Mooney nodded. "He didn't have the courage or skills to try again, so he took the coward's way out. You know, I'd forgotten about that until you mentioned his name. Serves the thug right. The world's better off without him."

That sounded a bit too callous for Brandon's liking, but he didn't want to make an issue of it. "How about the others?" he asked. "Did they finally realize that they'd picked on the wrong person?"

"Oh, yes," Mooney assured him with a smile. "Some of them I made certain would remember me. Andrew Daley, for example. Remember him?"

Brandon couldn't forget Andy Daley. The boy had picked on him mercilessly in the fifth grade. "Yeah. He moved away last year, and I finally got some peace."

"He's going to own a chain of stores in about twenty years' time, and do fairly well for himself," Mooney explained.

"That doesn't seem fair," Brandon complained.

"My thought exactly," the old man said. "So I bankrupted him." He smiled. "It felt good to see him crawl, Brandon. To finally pay him back after all those years."

Brandon nodded. It *did* sound good. But it also sounded . . . kind of extreme. He wasn't sure he really wanted to go that far in getting even. On the other hand, if that's what he did, then obviously it *was* right. Or he would never do it.

"And how about Brianne Waite?" Mooney suggested, a sly smile on his face. "You want to know what happens to her?"

"Brianne?" Brandon's face flushed as he thought about her. "The school babe? She's probably the rudest of all to me. Yeah, I'd love to know what happens to her."

Mooney laughed. "She marries you, Brandon."

"*Marries*?" He snorted. "There's no way she'd ever do that."

"Yes, there is," his older self answered. "She doesn't like you much, but she loves money. And you're going to be very, very rich. So when you go looking for her, she's suddenly very glad to see you. She's married by then, to a man in a dead-end job. You offer to take her away from all that, so she divorces her husband and marries you."

Brandon could think of worse fates than being married to such a total fox. "It sounds cool," he admitted. "So she loves me—in the future?"

"Don't be absurd," Mooney snapped. "She loved your *money*. The power. The parties. She never cared for me . . . you. But I knew that. And once she became addicted to the lifestyle, I divorced her, cut her off without a penny. Idiot that she was, she signed a prenuptial agreement that left her with nothing. I threw her away, having shown her everything she ever wanted—and then taken it all back. She learned how stupid she'd been."

Once again, Brandon felt very uncomfortable. This old man—*himself*—seemed to be very bitter and sadistic. Oh, true—he would have liked to pay Brianne back for being nasty. But there were limits to how far he'd go to achieve that goal. To deliberately wreck her marriage, show her the world and then throw her out in the trash seemed . . . extreme.

He was having a hard time understanding himself. But, he supposed, the difference came from eighty more years of life than he had now. Maybe other things would happen that would change him, make him tougher. "And what about Toni Frost?" he asked.

"Who?" Mooney's face was blank. "I don't remember anyone of that name. Who is he?"

"She," Brandon corrected. "She's a girl in my class. Short, dark hair, with a real attitude. She's started hanging around me today, and she won't leave me in peace."

Mooney shook his head. "She doesn't ring a bell," he replied, puzzled. "But I can't remember *everyone* after eighty years. She probably dries up and blows away. She certainly didn't do anything to annoy me enough for me to remember her."

"Oh." Again, Brandon wasn't sure how he felt about this. In one way, it was a relief to know she wouldn't be bothering him after this. But in another . . . Well, he kind of liked the fact that she was paying attention to him. Oh, she was annoying, too, but at least she didn't mock him. Well, not in the same way the other kids did. She seemed to think he was OK to hang out with, and it had been a long time since anyone else had ever thought that.

Brandon was still trying to make sense of everything. It was something of a whirlwind in his mind right now. Ideas and thoughts had been torn up, like the tree they were next to, exposing some strange things in his mind. "So you came back to meet me—yourself," he said slowly. "Why? I guess you remember being my age and this meeting taking place?"

"No," Mooney said firmly. "It never happened in my past. I simply grew up."

"Huh?" Brandon stared at him, lost again. "But if you're talking to me now, I *know* this isn't something I'm just going to forget about. No way. So you *must* remember meeting you when you were my age?''

''No,'' Mooney repeated. ''You see, I'm not *creating* the past. I'm *rewriting* it.'' He saw Brandon's blank look. ''OK, try this: I've returned to the past to alter the way it will happen. Remember I said I invented the time-field generator for a specific reason? Well, that reason was so that I could travel back in time and alter things. I don't want the future I come from to happen.''

Brandon was completely lost. ''I don't get it,'' he admitted. ''This meeting we're having never happened? You're trying to change things?''

''Not *trying*,'' Mooney replied. ''I *have* changed things. Whatever actions I take here and now alter the flow of history. I've changed time now on six different occasions. If I were to return to my own time now, it would be a very different place from when I left it. And just by talking to you like this, I'm changing the future again. When I was your age, I knew I was destined for greatness. I just didn't know what sort of greatness. Now I've told you, and you *do* know. Maybe now you'll invent the crystal lattices even earlier in your career, and maybe the time-field generator earlier, too. I haven't a clue yet.''

''OK,'' Brandon said slowly. ''I think I'm starting to understand some of this, at least. You want to change the world you live in. But *why*?''

''There's only one way to make you understand that,'' Mooney informed him. ''On your feet.'' They both got off the trunk, and the old man opened it up. It was filled with smaller cases. ''I brought back with me everything I thought I might need,'' he explained. ''This all helps me on my mission.'' He fished out one box and opened it. Inside was nestled something that looked like a huge bullet. He removed it carefully. ''This is a virtual reality generator,'' Mooney explained. ''It's hooked to a projection unit that I left in my own time. Put it on, and you'll see what my world is like. Then I'll explain what I'm doing here.'' He held out the Helmet.

Taking it, Brandon looked at it first. It seemed to have circuit boards on the inside, layered with some sort of greenish crystals. Obviously his own invention. Well, there was nothing much to worry about, then. It had to be safe. He took a deep breath, and donned the Helmet.

It was pitch black for a second, and then it was as if he was standing inside an office somewhere. Everything looked real enough to reach out and touch. He could feel the Helmet resting on his shoulders, but it wasn't visible.

It was a nice office. A black desk was in front of him, with some kind of recessed computer panel. There was a large screen on one wall, showing vague, shifting patterns. A couple of pieces of artwork stood on pedestals about the room, and there were several low, comfortable chairs.

''Turn around,'' he heard Mooney's voice say, vaguely muffled through the helmet. Brandon obeyed, and discovered that he was gazing out through a large picture window.

The view appalled him.

It looked like a desert that had been deliberately trashed. There was a naked hill, overlooking a dirty-colored stream. There was nothing living to be seen anywhere. The sky was dark and dismal.

''It's . . . horrible,'' he said, shocked.

The Helmet was lifted from his shoulders, and he was back in the woods again. Mooney nodded. ''It's terrible. And, since

I'm one of the richest men in the world, that's a lot nicer view than that which faces most of my contemporaries every single day of their wretched lives."

"How can people live like that?" asked Brandon, appalled.

"They can't, and they shouldn't." Mooney had replaced the Helmet and closed the trunk. "That's what I'm here to change. I know what caused such devastation, and I want to alter it forever. I want my world to become beautiful, a place that's worth living in. Not a desiccated wasteland."

Brandon nodded. "I can see that," he said. "It sounds like a great idea, and I'll do anything I can to help. But what caused all of that?" He gestured around him. "I mean, I know we have some environmental problems now, but they're nothing like what you're facing."

"They aren't—yet." Mooney sighed. "The problem is that people aren't always very logical. They trade sense for expediency. Many people are greedy, and they don't think that their small bits of greed will affect the future in any great way. They're not dreadfully evil, but their petty vices are enough to cause trouble." He seemed to change the subject for a moment. "Have you heard about Henry Brandt?"

Brandon had to think. "Uh, yeah. There was something in the news this morning about him having died last night. He's supposed to be a zillionaire, or something."

"Right," Mooney agreed. "He was also an industrialist who wanted to undercut some of the existing environmental laws. They were cutting into his profits. So he was going to buy off politicians and get the laws weakened. In that way, he would get what he wanted, and the Earth would become polluted. He simply didn't care."

Brandon was starting to get lost again. "I don't get it. Your world is polluted anyway. And he can't have done all of that, because he died last night.''

"In the world I came from, he *did* do that," Mooney explained. "Like I said, I came back to prevent that world from happening. I made certain that Brandt would never do what he had planned. I killed him last night.''

Brandon sat down on the chest with a thump. "You *killed* him?''

"Yes." Mooney saw him flinch away in horror. "Believe me, Brandon, it was the only thing I could do. I had to stop him.''

"Couldn't you have just *talked* to him?" Brandon cried. "Shown him what you just showed me? If he *knew*, then he'd never have done what he did.''

Mooney shook his head. "That's a lovely thought, but it's just so naive. Believe me, I didn't enjoy killing Brandt. But he would never have listened to me. He'd have never *seen* me, for one thing. People as rich as him don't just see anyone who walks in off the street. And he'd never have believed my story about being a time traveler.''

"You could have shown him the Helmet," Brandon protested.

"He would have called it a trick," Mooney insisted. "And then, if he'd believed me, he would have wanted to use me, to get me to tell him how to make himself even richer. How to change the future for *his* benefit, not the human race's.'' He leaned forward earnestly. "Believe me because I *know*. The first person I approached, I tried to do exactly what you suggested. He finally believed me, and was going to lock me up until I helped him to change the future so that he'd become the virtual ruler of the world. I had no choice but to kill him.''

"The *first* person?" Brandon echoed. "How many people have you killed?"

"Henry Brandt was the sixth," Mooney admitted.

Brandon was stunned. He was going to grow up to become a *killer*. He couldn't believe it; he didn't want to believe it. But there he was, sitting and watching him, and admitting to killing six people. Then a thought came to him. "It didn't work, did it?" he asked. "Killing them hasn't changed anything, has it?"

"Yes," Mooney said heavily. "It seems to have made things worse. But I can't just give up. I *have* to alter the future to give the human race a chance. That's why I came to you, Brandon. I need your help. You're of this time, and maybe you understand it a bit better than I do. Maybe you can help me with my job. Perhaps together we can change the course of the future."

Brandon was still trying to take all of this in. "So what is it you want me to do?" he asked faintly.

"I want you to join me on my crusade," Mooney explained enthusiastically. "Together, the two of us. I want you to help me pick out the next person that must die."

Brandon simply stared at him in horror. Mooney wanted *him* to become a killer, too . . .

CHAPTER 5

I KNOW THIS isn't an easy choice for you to make," Mooney said sympathetically. "After all, it wasn't an easy choice for *me* to make, and I'm you with eighty years' more experience. But we're enough alike for me to believe that you can understand me."

"No," Brandon told him. "We're *not* enough alike. I think that killing people is *wrong*, for whatever reason." He couldn't stomach the thought.

"Hitler," Mooney said simply.

"What?" Brandon glowered at him. "What are you talking about?"

"It's an old question," Mooney answered. "If you were taken back in time and shown the child who would one day grow up to become Adolf Hitler—who would one day plunge the world into total war; who would order the murder of millions of Jews, Gypsies and other *undesirables* in concentration camps—if you were shown him as a child, knowing what he would grow up to do, would you kill him?''

Brandon hesitated for a moment. He'd been studying the Holocaust in school, and knew of its terrible evils. To be able to prevent that from happening, even if it *was* by killing a child—wouldn't it be worth it? Or would the price be too great to pay? Brandon simply didn't know. He could see both sides of the question, and knew that he didn't have the experience with which to judge. "I don't know," he admitted miserably. "It sounds reasonable, but *is* it?" He shook his head. "It's too confusing for me."

Mooney patted him on the shoulder. "It's okay," he said. "Think it over tonight. I know it's a very hard decision for you to make. I'll see you here after school tomorrow, and then we can talk some more." He smiled. "Just remember— you've got a great future ahead of you. *If* we can cure the problems of my world."

Brandon nodded, and then hurried home. He needed to be left alone, to have time to think. What Mooney was asking him to do went against his beliefs. To kill someone, for whatever reason, had to be wrong, didn't it?

And then he remembered that bleak landscape of the future, where nothing could live. How could it be wrong to want to prevent that from happening by any means possible? If a man or two had to die in the process, didn't the end justify the means?

Brandon didn't know. He was only twelve years old—he shouldn't have to be facing a moral dilemma like this! So he did the only thing he could: he tried to forget about it for now. There was no point in trying to talk it over with his parents. They were okay, he supposed, but they were really out of touch sometimes. They wouldn't understand. What he needed was to talk about it to someone else, someone whose opinions he could trust. But he didn't have any friends at all. Most of the people he knew didn't want to hang around with him. And, to be honest, he didn't want to have anything to do with them, either. They were all stupid, and interested only in sports or TV or other mindless activities.

Instead, he thought about what his future was going to be like. His older self had said he'd become really famous, a brilliant inventor, and become very rich. That all sounded like it could be very appealing. He'd certainly not say no to any of that! And marrying Brianne Waite sounded neat, too. She was *definitely* the most beautiful girl imaginable.

But then there was that downside. Mooney had said that he'd marry Brianne only to get his revenge on her, and then he'd dump her, penniless, into the gutter. Maybe she deserved that; she'd been really nasty to him, after all. But wasn't that kind of extreme? His older self sounded like he enjoyed getting back at people who had hurt him.

Brandon had to admit that there was definitely an appeal to the idea of hurting people like Rory Tucker back. The bully deserved something for this morning's bloody nose, and for all the other times he'd picked on Brandon. But, again, ruining his life and pushing him into committing suicide seemed to be rather extreme. Though if Rory were so weak that he'd kill himself just because his business failed, he was an even weaker character than Brandon had previously thought.

Still, revenge is sweet . . . Brandon couldn't help feeling a thrill when he thought that Brianne and Rory would pay for their horrible behavior toward him. Whatever happened to them was their own fault, not really his. If they'd only been nicer to him, he wouldn't have to teach them a lesson. . . .

It was still too much for him to really be able to take in. He decided to sleep on the issue, and try to make a decision at school tomorrow. Brandon slept badly, tossing and turning, and by morning he hardly felt rested. He set off for school in a bad mood.

It wasn't improved when he saw Toni Frost. She'd obviously been waiting for him, and she fell in beside him as he walked the last couple of blocks to school. "So," she asked cheerily, "did you get whatever it was you had to do yesterday done? Are we going for pizza today?"

He gave her a filthy look. "Can't you take a hint?" he asked rudely. "I don't want anything to do with you. Isn't that clear enough?"

"Somebody got up in a bad mood this morning," Toni answered, not at all put off. "Or is it just that you're broke? If you like, I'll pay for the pizza."

"You just don't get it, do you?" he snapped. "It's not the money. It's that I don't want to hang around with you. Leave me alone."

"So you can be all grouchy?" she asked. "You can't spend your life like that. You're missing out on so much. Be adventurous—do something different for a change. Make up your mind to have some fun." She cocked her head and looked at him. "Do you know, I've never seen you smile. You might look a lot better if you did. Why don't you try it?"

His temper was curdling now. "Because I've got nothing to be happy about," he told her. "Why don't you leave me alone? That would cheer me up."

"Nonsense," Toni answered. "There's lots to make you happy. For example, look at that adorable little dog."

He looked where she was pointing. There was a small West Highland terrier, rolling on its back in a garden, feet waving in the air. "He's happy," Toni explained. "Nothing complicated, just enjoying the world. If he can do it, you can." She grinned. "If you want to roll on your back and kick your legs in the air, I promise not to tell anyone."

"He's just a dumb dog," Brandon snapped. "I hate animals. And I'm certainly not going to start acting like one to amuse you."

Toni sighed. "You can't really *hate* animals," she said. "They're lovable. How can you not like a dog like that?"

Brandon snorted. "All dogs want is food and some dumb toy to play with. They take from you, and give nothing in return. Why would I want something like that?"

"Nothing?" Toni glared at him. He'd finally managed to say something that had annoyed her. "They give affection and loyalty. Nobody is alone if they have a dog who loves them. But you don't even have that, do you? You're such a miserable human being, you know that?"

"If I'm so bad, you don't want to hang around with me, then," Brandon retorted. "I might infect you."

Toni shook her head. "Quite the opposite, Brandon Mooney. I'm hanging around you so that I can infect *you*. You see, I happen to know that there's a pretty nice person inside you somewhere. He's just been buried under a whole mountain of anger, resentment and hurt. I'm staying right with you until he can dig his way out again."

"You'll have a long wait, then," Brandon told her. He resented her attempts to psychoanalyze him. Anyway, she was completely wrong about him. He wasn't like that at all.

"Then I'll wait," she replied simply. "But it won't take very long. All you have to do is let go of all that anger and simply start doing nice things for other people. The next thing you know, you might even start enjoying life."

Brandon rolled his eyes. What a simplistic philosophy! He wasn't even sure why he was arguing with her, except that he didn't want her to think she'd won the argument if he simply stopped talking. "I am *not* filled with anger."

"Of course you are," Toni said. "You're so angry that if someone gave you a gun and stood you next to Rory Tucker, you'd kill him. Wouldn't you?"

Brandon was suddenly shocked speechless. It was almost as if Toni had figured out what had been going through his mind. That was impossible, of course; she was just using cheap psychological tricks she'd probably read in some magazine to try to figure him out. She was wrong, of course, but she'd actually managed to get pretty close to the problem that was really bothering him.

"I don't believe it's right to kill people," he finally said. "No matter what the provocation."

"Well, I'm glad you believe in *something*," she told him. "It's not much, but it's a start. Maybe we can build on that and bring a decent human being out from inside you. The next thing you have to do is to realize that killing people springs from hatred, and then get rid of all that resentment and hatred that's festering inside of you. If you don't, one day it's going to explode."

Ignoring her silly comment, Brandon focused on the one thing in what she'd said that interested him. "Killing people doesn't always spring from hatred,'' he told her. ''Sometimes you can kill people for good reasons.''

''Really?'' She snorted. ''Like in a war, you mean, where it's okay to kill another human being simply because he's on the opposite side to you?''

''Maybe that,'' Brandon replied. ''But I was thinking of killing someone for a positive reason.'' She was irritating, but maybe she could help him think through what was bothering him. ''Look, let's suppose that somehow you could see into the future. And you discover that, say, Rory Tucker was going to become a general and start World War Three. And that this would wipe out the whole human race. And now, you're here, and Rory Tucker hasn't grown up yet. If you killed him today, you'd stop World War Three and save the human race. Wouldn't that be an example of killing someone for a good reason?''

''Boy, you're reaching,'' Toni answered. ''I think that the answer's still no. You can't get to a good end through a bad means. It doesn't work out. Using bad means will poison the end. Even if you saved the world, you're still a murderer. So maybe the world's better off, but you aren't. And anyway, you can't know that killing Rory would stop World War Three. Maybe instead of Rory, *you'd* then grow up and become the general who starts it. The war might well happen because of the general condition of the human race, not just because of one person's actions.''

He hadn't thought about it like that before, but he realized that she had a good point. ''So you're saying that if somebody had killed Hitler, it might not have stopped World War Two?'' he asked her.

''It *might* have,'' she answered. ''But I doubt it. Look, Hitler didn't act alone. There were a lot of people who worked with him—Goebbels and Bormann and others. If Hitler hadn't led the Third Reich, maybe one of them would have. It was the whole social climate of Germany at the time that gave rise to the war, not just one maniac ranting and raving. Oh, I'm sure he helped, but it wasn't *just* him." She gave a little shudder. "In fact, there's a little bit of Hitler in all of us, you know? Thinking that we know what's best for everyone, if they only listen to us. Thinking that prejudice is OK in some situations. Sometimes it's kind of easy to give in to these feelings. But we shouldn't."

Brandon stared at her in amazement. His bad mood had begun to lift as he'd listened to her. He realized that she was right. Killing Hitler wasn't really the solution to ending war. It wasn't just one man to blame, but a lot of different factors.

That had to be why his older self wasn't winning his war against polluting the planet. He was taking one small person at a time instead of trying to see the larger picture. Toni's comments were starting to make sense of it all to him.

She mistook his silence, though. "Yeah, I know. You probably think I'm just some dumb girl who should keep her opinions to herself, right?"

"No," he told her, feeling his lips twitching up into a smile. "On the contrary, Toni. I think what you just said makes a whole lot of sense. It's something I wish I'd thought of for myself."

She blinked, puzzled but pleased. "Brandon Mooney, I do believe you're smiling. Maybe there is hope for you after all. I just wish I knew what I did right. I mean, you weren't seriously thinking about killing Rory to save the future, were you?"

"Nothing like that, no," he assured her. "But there was something really bothering me that you've helped me with." He took a plunge, and added, "Maybe I *will* treat you to pizza, after all. But it can't be today. I've got to do something after school. How about tomorrow instead?"

Toni looked amazed, but she nodded. "It's a date." Then she grinned. "I mean *date* as in time, of course," she added. "Not as in a boy/girl thing. I wouldn't want to scare you off."

Brandon looked at her with fresh respect. They'd reached the school now, and he had to head off to class. "Maybe it wouldn't scare me," he told her, and then hurried off. He was rather surprised by his own words. And even more surprised to discover that he meant them. His first impressions about Toni had been wrong. She wasn't such an idiot, after all. In fact, now that he thought about it, she was actually pretty smart. Maybe even as smart as he was.

With his mood lightened, he felt much better at school. At lunchtime, Toni joined him. To his surprise, Brandon discovered that this didn't bother him at all. In fact, he rather enjoyed talking to her. Actually, she did most of the talking, and he listened. But she was interesting, and passionate about a lot of causes. She was almost able to convince him to join the National Wildlife Federation and help save the wolves.

After school, he hurried back to the woods and his little "cave."

Mooney was already there, waiting for him. The old man looked eager. "I'm glad you came back, Brandon," he said cheerfully. "So, have you decided to join me in saving my world?"

"No," Brandon informed him. "Because I don't think the way you're doing it will work."

The old man's smile was wiped away. "But I was *sure* you'd come to realize that I'm right," he said, almost sulkily. "I *have* to save my time from its fate. Surely you can agree that this is a goal worth working toward?"

"A hundred percent," agreed Brandon. "By any other means than killing people." He took a deep breath. "I've been talking to this girl at school, and she convinced me that it's not a simple matter to change the future. I thought about what she said, and I've come to the conclusion she's right."

"She's corrupted you," Mooney growled.

"No, she hasn't," Brandon insisted. "She's helped me to get it all straight in my head. Look, you're seeing pollution and decay in your world, and you've traced it back to one man doing one thing. You think that killing him will stop it from happening. But it *won't*!"

"Of course it will," Mooney argued. "Like Brandt. His firms polluted my world, and killing him should have stopped it."

"But it didn't," Brandon pointed out. "And I can tell you why. Because maybe whoever took over after Brandt died had the same ideas and aims as Brandt. So *he* would have done what Brandt did. And so things didn't change. Besides which, Brandt only managed to pollute the world to death because he bought off a couple of politicians. Killing Brandt doesn't stop them from being corrupt. If he didn't bribe them, then somebody else probably did. And so, the same thing still happens: your world gets polluted to death. Killing Brandt didn't change anything. And it can't."

Mooney shook his head stubbornly. "You're wrong," he insisted. "You have to be. I can't believe that there isn't any hope for my world. I *can't*! And I won't let it just happen because you've decided that it's hopeless to fight.'' He glared at Brandon. ''I had hoped that you'd help me, but if you won't, then stay out of my way. I'm going to save my world, even if you won't do a thing to help me.''

Brandon stared at him, realizing that he hadn't gotten through to the older man. ''You're planning on killing someone else, aren't you?'' he realized.

''Yes.'' Mooney glowered at him. ''A man called Troy Ryder. I've checked my reference book, and in eight years, he's going to cause a huge oil spill in the Alaskan National Forest that will wipe out virtually all wildlife there. It will pollute the waters and result in thousands of Eskimos dying. The whole area will be uninhabitable forever. Maybe *you* don't care, but I do. And I'm going make absolutely certain that it doesn't happen.''

Brandon opened his mouth to argue, but Mooney touched his belt, and simply vanished.

He'd used his time-field generator to move away from the present. He was going to kill someone else.

CHAPTER 6

BRANDON DIDN'T KNOW what he should do. Mooney had obviously gone off to kill Troy Ryder, in another attempt to change the future. He'd been very annoyed with Brandon for refusing to help out, but there was no way that Brandon could do so with a clear conscience. He couldn't see that killing anyone would help.

But now he knew that Mooney was going through with his plan, if he *didn't* do something, he'd be an accessory before the fact. Brandon was pretty sure that was the correct legal term. If he didn't try to stop Mooney, it would be as bad as helping him. But how could you possibly stop someone who could travel in time?

There was only one thing that Brandon could think of: he'd have to warn the police that somebody was trying to kill this Ryder, whoever he was. The problem was, he felt like a trai-

tor, betraying his older self like this. What if the police caught
Mooney and locked him up? Then what? Brandon was getting
more and more confused as he thought about the problem. He
didn't really want to have his older self arrested, but what else
could he do? He couldn't simply sit back and let the murder
go through.

Brandon hurried out of the woods and started for home. He
had to call the police.

And then he stopped. They'd want to know who he was,
and how he knew that a murder was being planned. He really
didn't want to tell them his name. If they caught Mooney,
they might then start wondering who he was. He'd even have
the same fingerprints.

So he'd have to make it an anonymous call. Only, if he
called from home, he was sure that the police could trace the
call to his house, which would defeat the purpose of not giving his name. So he'd have to use a public phone. And a call
to 911 didn't cost anything. He thought for a minute, and
remembered there was a phone outside the pizza parlor in the
strip mall near school. That would be perfect.

It took him only ten minutes to get there. The pizza place
was quite busy, since it was a favorite hangout of the school
crowd. There was some kid he vaguely knew using the phone,
so Brandon was forced to wait impatiently until he was finished. Then he snatched up the phone and dialed 911. When
the operator came on, he asked for the police. There was a
knot of tension and fear in his stomach. He was *almost* sure
he was doing the right thing . . . but he still felt very bad about
it.

"I want to report a murder," he told the police operator
when she came on.

"Someone has been killed?" the operator asked.

"Not yet," he said. "At least, I don't think so. It's a man called Troy Ryder. Do you know who he is?"

"No," the operator answered. "Can you give me some details?"

"Not really," Brandon answered. "All I know is that I heard this man saying he was going to kill a Troy Ryder tonight. I think he must live around here somewhere, but I don't know where."

"I see." There was a slight pause. "I need to have some information," she told him. "What's your name and address?"

Uh-oh. The knot in his stomach twisted a couple more turns. "Uh, I'd rather not say," he told her.

"I see." There was distinct suspicion in her voice now. "And who was this man you overheard? Can you tell me his name, or what he looks like?"

Ouch! "Uh, I don't know his name," he lied. "But he's about six feet tall, with grayish hair. He looks about sixty years old. He's dressed completely in black."

There was another pause, and then the operator said, "Listen, young man. You're calling from a public phone near a pizza parlor. We've had several prank calls from there before. If you won't give me your name and address, I'm going to have to assume that this is simply another one of them. You school kids should know better than to make hoax calls to nine-one-one."

"This isn't a hoax!" Brandon exclaimed. "You've got to believe me! Troy Ryder is in danger of being murdered! You've got to warn him, and protect him. You've *got* to!"

"We will," the operator said. "But we'd feel a lot better about it if you'd just give us your name."

Then Brandon realized something that scared him. She *knew* where he was calling from! She'd traced the call. He was willing to bet anything that she'd also sent out a police car to check on who was using the phone. She was just trying to keep him talking until they found him! He slammed the phone down, and looked wildly around. Then he moved fast, heading for the stationery store next to the pizza parlor. As he did so, another boy came out of the pizza parlor and went to the phone. Brandon stood inside the store, looking out through the window.

Less than twenty seconds later, a police car pulled into the lot. A policeman came out and crossed to where the other boy was on the phone.

It had been a close call! They were bound to realize that they had the wrong person once they talked to this kid. And then another thought came to Brandon: the boy must have seen Brandon at the phone; he might be able to tell the police what Brandon looked like. And he might remember seeing Brandon go into the stationery store . . .

Brandon's palms started to sweat as he saw the policeman approach the other boy. He could really be in trouble any moment now.

And then the boy on the phone saw the policeman. He dropped the receiver, turned and ran. The policeman sprinted after him.

What was going on? Brandon couldn't believe his eyes. This was really weird. There was a movement beside him, and a girl a couple of years older than Brandon was staring out the window next to him. She gave a short laugh as she saw the policeman grab the fleeing kid.

"Serves him right," she commented. "We all knew the cops would get Larry one of these days."

Brandon was puzzled. "What's he done?"

The girl gave him a grin. "He's always making prank calls and irritating people. It looks like he didn't get off the line fast enough this time." She shrugged, and went back to checking out the teen magazines.

It was an incredible relief. The police had caught a genuine hoax caller! They wouldn't come looking for Brandon, then, and he was safe. The boy would obviously deny he'd made the call about Troy Ryder. But would the police believe him? Or would they just assume Brandon's call had been a joke? If they did, then this Troy Ryder wouldn't be warned.

Brandon couldn't take the chance. He needed to check out the phone book, and see if he could call the man himself and warn him. He waited until the policeman had placed the boy in his car, and then watched him drive away. Then he dashed out of the store and hurried home.

His parents weren't home yet, of course, so he checked out the local phone book. There was nobody listed by the name of Troy Ryder. Now what? Then he remembered that his father had one of those discs of phone numbers for his computer. He was an insurance salesman, and often needed them. He hurried into the study, and booted up the computer. Once it was going, he checked out the disc.

Still no entry for Troy Ryder. There were a couple of T. Ryders, but he had no way of telling if either might be a Troy. And one was in California, the other in Idaho. They seemed a bit far away. Mooney had specifically mentioned that he could only travel in time, not space. So he had to be hunting for someone who lived close by. Brandon slammed his hand down on the desk in frustration. He was trying so hard to do the right thing, but nothing seemed to be working. He'd simply run out of ideas now.

Whatever happened next, he'd done his best.

He just hoped he could live with it.

Mooney had located Ryder's house without much trouble. Like Brandt, Ryder preferred to keep a low profile. He had a large house in spacious grounds for himself and his family. There was also, Mooney noted, a small army of retainers and hangers-on about the place. Where Brandt had been a recluse, Ryder was a party animal.

It was now after dark, but the house was just starting to come to life. Cars were arriving and dropping guests off. Mooney was watching from across the road, perched in another tree, his field glasses focused on the front door of the Ryder house. This was certainly going to be some party tonight. And, according to his Book, this was a fairly common event. Ryder was gregarious, and really enjoyed meeting people.

It wasn't simply showing off, either. The man was a charitable donor, and the chances were that this was a party to raise funds for AIDS research, or else to save some endangered species of animal. Mooney found this particularly ironic, since Ryder's companies were already polluting the world and would contribute to the rise in toxic deaths over the next quarter-century. And Ryder was apparently oblivious to his own hypocrisy, clearly thinking that he was doing good with his charitable functions while committing private sins that more than outweighed the good. People were astonishingly adept at placating their own consciences sometimes.

But Ryder's do-good times were no more than a Band-Aid on the festering sore of his real contributions to the human race. And Mooney simply couldn't allow him to continue the way he was going.

By the look of things, this party was just getting warmed up. Mooney could hear the faint strains of some antique big-band music being played live in the house. It would last for several hours yet. Anyone else would have had a long, tiring wait ahead of them. Mooney simply set his belt controls to take him four hours into the future.

His vision wavered slightly and then cleared. Now the stars were out, and the air a trifle more chilled. But the party seemed to be still going. Well, let Ryder enjoy his last night on Earth. He set the controls for another shift of two hours.

This time, when his vision cleared, he could see that he'd timed it better. It was almost three in the morning, and several cars were pulling away from the house. Excellent. Some of the lights had been turned off, and there was a knot of people by the front door clearly waiting their turn to leave. Almost perfect.

Mooney set his next jump for a half hour and a spatial shift that would land him at the back of the house. Ryder's bedroom was on the second story, right above the ballroom where the party had been held. There was a momentary shimmer in his vision as usual, and Mooney arrived on the back lawn in the same prone position he'd held in the tree.

He rose to his feet, surveying the house with a tight smile. The spatial shift had enabled him to avoid any security devices that might already be armed. Of course, if Ryder had guard dogs, they would be a problem. But there was another large, ornamental tree close by, and he quickly climbed it. This one overlooked the portion of the house that he wanted.

There was a light on in the correct bedroom. Obviously Ryder had set his servants to work cleaning up from the party and then retired. Unlike Brandt, Ryder got along well with his wife, so she'd most likely be in the room, too. Mooney felt a twinge of guilt that she'd have to watch her husband die, but he suppressed the feeling. It was nothing really personal. His mission came first, and that meant that Ryder simply had to die. It was no more than unfortunate that Mrs. Ryder would be present.

Mooney watched the room through his field glasses. It wouldn't do to hit the wrong person. The curtains were drawn, so he switched the viewing mode to infrared. The shift was instant, and he could see straight through the curtains. And just about everything else in the room, too. The glasses compensated for the usual distortion that infrared would cause. A small microprocessor converted the images so that it looked as if he were simply observing in normal light.

Except, of course, for the fact that it only picked up heat. This meant that clothing was invisible to him. He was watching Ryder and his wife in the buff. Mrs. Ryder held a glowing cup, presumably coffee or hot chocolate, which was incredibly intense in this mode of viewing. Mooney switched from her to her husband immediately. He wasn't here as a Peeping Tom, but as an assassin, after all.

Ryder was clearly getting ready for bed, which didn't leave Mooney much time. He could fire through the curtains, but not through brick walls. He took out his rifle, and switched on the power cell. This, too, had the infrared adapter, and he trained on his target through it. Ryder was moving to open the window slightly for some fresh air. Perfect!

As Ryder gripped the window, Mooney fired.

The rifle he was using was a marvelous device. It fired a point electrical pulse; all Mooney had to do was aim it at his victim's head. When the pulse hit, it would create a massive cerebral hemorrhage that killed instantly. It would look in any autopsy as if the victim had simply suffered a massive stroke. Nobody would ever suspect murder.

Ryder stiffened, his mouth opening in a scream that Mooney, thankfully, couldn't hear. Then he fell backward, into his room. Through the sights, Mooney saw Mrs. Ryder drop her cup and dash to her husband's side in panic.

He sighed. It was a shame that he had to kill the man, and he felt sympathy for the new widow. But he couldn't allow his emotions to interfere with his mission. He shut down the rifle, and replaced it over his shoulder. Then he reset the belt controls to take him back across country to his base in the woods.

Once again, he found himself prone in the dirt. He straightened up, brushing soil from his suit, and turned to where he had left his equipment. This time, it *had* to have worked properly. He *must* have made the changes he wanted. His world *had* to be safe! With trembling fingers, he lifted the Helmet from its box and held it ready. He was almost afraid to slip it on. What if nothing had changed again? Could he accept yet another failure? But what option did he have? He had to see what had happened, even if it was nothing. Steeling himself, he pulled on the Helmet.

Light flared all around him, and he was looking out from his office once again.

It had definitely changed this time.

He was looking out of a shattered wall, across a dried-up riverbed at the hillside. Gray dust covered everything, blowing slightly in a stiff breeze.

There was no sign of a single living creature, nor a single blade of grass.

He was looking out over an Earth that wasn't simply dead; it had been sterilized . . .

Mooney pulled the Helmet off with a cry of rage and shock. It had happened again. He'd changed the future once more, and this time for the very worst: his world was not simply polluted and dying now.

It was completely, utterly dead.

CHAPTER 7

BRANDON FELT DREADFUL. He'd spent a restless night worrying about matters he had absolutely no control over. He knew in his heart that he'd done the best he could, and that there wasn't really any blame to him if Mooney had somehow managed to kill Ryder after all. But it didn't help salve his conscience. Because, whether he liked it or not, Mooney was *him*. Which meant that he would one day grow up to be a murderer.

The thought haunted him. He realized that Mooney felt that he had no option but to kill in the hopes that he could make his world better. But that wasn't enough for Brandon.

Finally, he gave up even trying to sleep and got up. He was too early for school yet, which wasn't something that often happened. He had no appetite for breakfast, but he did have some juice to take the bad taste out of his mouth. He sat alone in the kitchen, his parents still sleeping, wondering what was going to happen to him.

What had turned him into Mooney? OK, he understood some of what was driving the man. But he seemed so intense, so focused on revenge, for example. Brandon didn't like Rory Tucker, but he couldn't imagine himself ever being glad that Rory had killed himself. But Mooney had been very glad. And the business with Brianne Waite. Mooney had married her—not out of love, or even lust; he'd done it to deliberately humiliate her. OK, maybe Brianne wasn't the nicest person in the world, but the thought of deliberately conning her like that made him feel sick.

Sure, he'd like to get back at both of them. But a *reasonable* revenge, not something so extreme. Brandon had fantasies in which he beat the tar out of Rory Tucker. He knew it would never happen—Rory was too big and athletic, and Brandon was skinny and used his hands on a computer keyboard—but it was nice to imagine bloodying Rory's nose. If anyone deserved to get a thrashing, it was Rory. But that was all. He didn't want the other boy dead.

And he definitely had fantasies about Brianne, but none of them involved breaking her spirit. Oh, he had one that he liked in which she decided she'd been wrong and begged him for a date, and he then casually turned her down, humiliating her in public. But to marry her only to wreck her . . .

What kind of monster *was* Mooney?

The problem was, Brandon *knew* the answer. Mooney was the monster that Brandon would grow into. And that meant that everything that he detested in Mooney was somewhere within him, too. It was already taking root, and would one day grow into Mooney.

He was doomed to become a sadistic, well-intentioned murderer.

Oh, and on the bright side, rich, famous and alone.

Brandon had often tried to imagine what his future would be. He'd had fantasies about success, wealth, and women fawning all over him, of course. Never once had he imagined that he could turn out like Mooney. Now he *knew* what his own future was; he knew what he would become.

And he loathed it.

Eventually, his parents got up, and he ate a little breakfast with them. As soon as he could, he left for school. He didn't really feel like it, but he needed something to distract him. He'd checked the obituaries in the newspaper, but hadn't found anything about a Troy Ryder. Of course, maybe it had happened too late to make the news. Or maybe Ryder wasn't considered important enough to report about.

Or, just maybe, maybe the police had taken his warning seriously after all. Maybe Ryder was still alive.

God, he hoped so. But he wasn't willing to believe it without some evidence. Much as he disliked the thought, Brandon knew that he'd have to go to the woods after school and see if Mooney was still there. And whether he had any news.

Brandon's stomach churned, and he wished he hadn't eaten any breakfast.

"Wow, you look really terrible this morning," a familiar female voice said.

Wincing, Brandon turned to see Toni hurrying to catch up with him. "Thanks," he said. "I really needed to hear that."

"So, what else are friends for?" she asked. "What's wrong? Homework trouble? Family trouble?"

"I don't want to talk about it," he told her. Oddly enough,

he discovered that he didn't feel quite so bad now that Toni was with him. Not that he was actually getting to *like* her, of course. But she was kind of easy to be around, even with her smart mouth.

"That's your problem," she snapped. "You don't want to talk about it. You don't want to talk about *anything*. You just bottle it up inside. And that's a big mistake, because it's like a volcano. If you don't let some of the pressure out, one day you'll just blow your top like Vesuvius, and everyone will get caught in the explosion."

The idea hit Brandon with almost physical force. He stopped dead in his tracks and stared at her. Did she have a point? Was that what had happened to turn Brandon into Mooney? Had Mooney been formed because Brandon had bottled everything up and then exploded?

"Say something," Toni pleaded. "Even tell me I'm an idiot, if you like. Just don't stand there like a statue, Brandon."

He blinked, and shook his head. "I was just thinking about what you said," he told her slowly. "Maybe you do have a point."

"I do?" She smiled slightly. "Sorry, sometimes I make sense. I try not to do it, but it happens anyway. Does that mean that you want to talk about your problems?"

"I don't know," he told her honestly. "To tell you the truth, if I told you what was bugging me, you'd probably think I'd already blown my top and was ready to have a brain transplant or something."

Toni gave him an odd look. "Oh, I don't know. I have a pretty open mind. It's so open, things sometimes fall out of the edges. But I'm not going to push you. If you want to talk,

I'll listen. If not, I'll just keep on talking to cover up the silence, OK?''

He couldn't help smiling. ''OK. Anyway, I promise you that if I decide to talk about it to anyone, it'll be you.''

''Thanks—I think.'' She shifted her backpack to her other shoulder. ''So, are you still on for after school?''

He'd forgotten about that. He'd promised her pizza, hadn't he? But that was when he thought he'd be finished with Mooney. ''I don't know,'' he answered. ''I'd like to, but . . .''

''But there's somewhere you have to go, something you need to do?'' Toni shook her head. ''I hope this isn't just your way of saying you don't want to be seen with me. I could always wear a disguise, you know.'' She grinned. ''You think I'd look good in a blond wig?''

She had this weird habit of making him think of things that hadn't occurred to him before. He looked at her and realized something. Toni Frost was actually rather attractive. Her short hair was maybe a bit masculine, and he rather preferred Brianne's flowing style. But she had a nice face and deep, interesting eyes. And she was certainly a lot brighter and more pleasant than Brianne. He tried to picture Toni with long blond hair, but it just wouldn't work. The blond look was fine for Brianne, but not Toni.

''I think you look good just the way you are,'' he told her.

She actually blushed slightly at this. ''You think so?'' She fingered her hair. ''You don't think maybe this is a bit short? My mom tells me it is.''

''Maybe it could stand a few more inches,'' he replied, knowing he was blushing slightly himself. ''But on you it looks good.''

''Maybe there's hope for me yet,'' Toni said. ''And maybe

even for you, too. Thanks for the compliment, Brandon.''

They had reached the school by now, and she gave him a wink and then hurried off to her locker. Brandon found himself watching her, not entirely understanding how he felt about her. It wasn't a hormone kind of thing, like with Brianne. After all, a guy would have to be blind not to notice someone like Brianne. But, on the other hand, there was just something about Toni that was kind of . . . comfortable.

"Hey, it looks like the doofus has got a girlfriend!"

Brandon winced. Just as it had seemed as if his life was taking a little upswing, it came crashing back down again. Rory Tucker, of course. And he couldn't just stay out of Brandon's life. Brandon ignored the voice, and continued walking toward his own locker. He had a hard time, though, because he could feel hostile eyes staring at him.

"So I'm not good enough to talk to now, hey, pond scum?"

Brandon knew that ignoring him wasn't going to work. He turned around and saw Rory glaring at him. Six other boys were hanging about with the big youth, ready to laugh or back him up. Classic pack mentality, he knew, with Rory as the alpha male.

"I just don't want to use big words," Brandon replied. "I know how anything with more than two syllables in it confuses you."

"You think you're funny?" Rory challenged.

Brandon sighed mentally. He *really* didn't want another confrontation with the bully, but it looked like Rory was intent on scoring some points. "Look," he said, trying to be reasonable, "if it will make your morning brighter to insult me, go ahead and do it. I'm sure your friends will laugh, even if it isn't funny. But I'm not interested, OK?'' He shrugged his shoulders and started to turn away.

That wasn't what Rory wanted. He thrust his hand out, shoving at Brandon's shoulder. "Don't smart-mouth me, you jackass," he growled. "You'd better apologize to me."

"For what?" asked Brandon. He could feel the tension in the air, and his stomach was already working itself into knots.

"Anything you like," Rory answered, grinning nastily. "I just want you to tell me you're sorry for what you did."

This was too much. Brandon shook his head. "Get a life," he advised the bully. "I know you can knock the stuffing out of me if you feel like it, and so do you. So does everyone else here. But I'm not going to grovel to you to try to avoid it."

Rory glared down at him. "You're talking mighty big this morning. Do you think your girlfriend will come back and save you again?"

"She's not my girlfriend," Brandon answered. "And I have absolutely no idea what she's likely to do. She's kind of independent, you know."

"She's an idiot to hang out with you," Rory growled. "She should hang out with a real man."

"Well, if you find any, maybe you should let her know," Brandon answered. "I'm sure she'd be grateful."

That one definitely didn't go down well with Rory, and Brandon almost wished he hadn't said it. But he was telling the truth: Rory could certainly take him anytime if he wanted to, but he wasn't going to bow down and kiss his sneakers to avoid a beating. Maybe a couple of punches would hurt, but humiliating himself like that would hurt more in the long run.

"How'd you like a knuckle sandwich?" Rory demanded.

"No, thanks," Brandon told him. "I'm on a restricted diet." That got a snigger from one of the other boys, and Rory glared him into silence.

"That Frost kid needs someone like me to show her a good time," Rory said. "Maybe I should volunteer. She certainly doesn't need a wimp like you."

Brandon snorted. "If you try, I think you'll end up singing soprano. She won't take any of your nonsense."

"Are you saying a *girl* could take me on?" Rory growled. He hauled his fist back and took a swing at Brandon.

But Brandon wasn't about to remain in the path of Rory's fist. He ducked to the side, and the punch whipped past his ear. "Calm down," he suggested, feeling the knot in his stomach turn into a heavy stone. "There's no need for violence."

"I'm going to fix you," Rory promised. "And then I'll see to Frost, too. She's going to regret even knowing you."

That was too much for Brandon. It was bad enough that Rory was picking on him, but now he was threatening Toni, too—simply because she was his friend. Something snapped inside Brandon's mind, and he stopped thinking logically. He dropped his backpack, and with a growl of anger he punched Rory back. It wasn't a very hard blow, and Rory's stomach was mostly muscle. But it was unexpected. Rory had been certain that Brandon would simply try to escape, and he hadn't anticipated a punch. His breath snorted out, and he hesitated for a second.

Brandon was beyond worrying now about getting hurt. Rory had threatened to hurt Toni, and Brandon wasn't going to stand for that. He swung a second blow at Rory, and then a third and fourth. None of them was at all scientific or even terribly effective as fighting. But they made Rory pause and realize that Brandon wasn't wimping out this time. Brandon didn't care; he just wanted to hurt Rory. His anger was too great for conscious thought; all he wanted to see was Rory lying on the ground in a pool of his own blood. He swung again and again, hardly even feeling surprised that Rory wasn't punching back. The bully had his hands up in defensive positions, taking most of Brandon's blows on the arms.

Brandon wasn't sure how long this lasted. There was a haze over his mind. He did feel one return blow, a lot harder than any he'd landed, across the left shoulder. All that did was to make him strike out wilder and harder. One of his punches smacked into Rory's nose, and there was a smear of blood on the other boy's face.

"Stop this immediately!"

Even through his haze, Brandon heard the authoritarian tones of Vice-Principal Marotta. He landed one last blow, and then let his hands fall to his sides. He was panting heavily, and there were several places where he hurt. His fists were almost numb, but his wrists hurt from the force of the blows he'd given. His mind was slowly clearing again. Rory, too, was panting, and he allowed his own hands to fall down.

Mr. Marotta came up to them. "Brawling in the corridors is not allowed, as I am sure the two of you are well aware." He glared at Rory, and then at Brandon. "I'm giving you both detention for Friday night. Now, get to your classes, all of you."

Brandon nodded, and picked up his backpack. His hands hurt as he gripped it and swung it over his right shoulder. His left hurt too much. Without a word, he turned and walked away.

Detention! He'd never had detention in his life. He felt

disgraced. And he also felt ashamed of what he had done. He had simply given in to the anger inside him and attacked Rory. Maybe the other boy had been looking for it, and had provoked it, but Brandon was shocked to discover that side to his nature. He'd always thought he was too smart to get into fights, but he had just learned something here: that there was plenty of anger inside him, just as Toni had observed, and that he was quite capable of letting it out. He had really wanted to hurt Rory Tucker for threatening Toni.

And that bothered him. Not that he was defending Toni; that felt OK. It was the anger he'd felt toward Rory that worried him. He'd really wanted to pound the other boy into pulp. He'd wanted to smash him, and he had felt really good when he'd bloodied Rory's nose in payback.

The problem was that Brandon could see where this was leading him. He'd tried to hurt Rory, and possibly succeeded. And he knew that there was still plenty of anger left inside him. Under the right circumstances, he'd do exactly the same thing over again. And that really scared him.

This was the kind of anger that Mooney felt. The anger that had driven him to hurt Rory Tucker, and to gloat when the adult Rory killed himself. The kind of anger that made him humiliate and break Brianne Waite.

Brandon had just seen the first stirrings of Mooney inside his own soul. And that scared him very badly indeed.

CHAPTER 8

SOMEHOW, BRANDON STUMBLED through classes until lunchtime. Then he retreated outside, wanting to be alone with his depression. Life was just getting worse and worse for him, and he wasn't sure how much more he could take. Tapping into the anger inside of him had felt so good while he was doing it. But now . . . now, all it did was make him realize the depths to which he could possibly plummet.

"Avoiding me, huh?" asked Toni.

Brandon looked up from where he was sitting under a tree, having to shade his eyes against the glare of the sun. "I'm avoiding everybody," he told her. "Except the one person I really want to avoid. Myself."

Toni sat down beside him. "Yeah. I heard you had another run-in with Rory Tucker this morning." She grinned. "And that this time, you were the one giving the bloody nose. I'm proud of you, Brandon.''

''Well, that makes one of us,'' he replied glumly.

Her eyes narrowed as she studied him. ''I don't get it. What's wrong with you? It's all over the school that you took on Rory, and that you almost looked like you were going to beat him. Doesn't that make you happy? Or is it that you've got detention, and it blemishes your perfect record?'' She shrugged. ''If that's it, then I'll go get detention, too, so at least you'll have a partner to share your misery with.''

Brandon could see that Toni was trying to cheer him up. The problem was that she really didn't have a clue as to what was really bugging him. ''It's not that. Frankly, I don't care about detention right now.''

''Then what is it?'' Toni glared at him. ''I thought you'd agreed that bottling things up inside you wasn't healthy. Come on, tell me what's wrong.''

''I don't think I agreed to make you my confessor,'' he snapped, a little harsher than he'd meant to. It was that temper of his again! ''I'm sorry, I didn't mean it like that,'' he apologized. ''But you *really* wouldn't understand what my problem is.''

''It's a boy thing, huh?'' Toni smiled. ''OK, I may not be a guy, but I've got a good imagination. I can *pretend* I'm a guy for a while. And so can you, if you try. Especially with this haircut. You know, I'm starting to agree with you and Mom; I think I should grow it out some.''

Brandon almost managed to smile at her weak attempt at humor. ''It's not a guy thing. In fact, as far as I know, it's something nobody else has ever gone through before.''

Toni raised her eyebrows. ''You've evolved some new kind

of mental anguish? Hey, I'm proud of you. Keep this up, and you'll get the Nobel Prize yet.'' Then she patted his arm. ''OK, maybe I *won't* understand. But you could try me. If I get out of my depth, I'll holler for a life belt, OK? Now, what's bothering you so much?''

Brandon focused on his feelings. He had to tell *somebody* what was wrong with him. And, to be honest, he did feel comfortable talking to Toni. He wasn't exactly sure why, but her persistence was getting through his barriers. ''You were right about the anger inside of me,'' he told her. ''When I was fighting Rory this morning, I wanted nothing more than to wipe the floor with his blood. And it scared the heck out of me.''

''Trust me, there are plenty of people who dream of wiping the floor with his blood,'' Toni assured him. ''He's one of the most unpopular people in the school. Most people don't have the guts to go up against him, but you did. That's nothing to be ashamed of. He asked for it, and you gave it to him. It'll be a while before he even thinks about picking on you again.''

''That's not the point,'' Brandon told her. ''I agree with you, Rory deserved to get his nose bloodied. That's not my problem. The problem is with *me*.'' He sighed, and lowered his voice. ''When I was fighting Rory, I got a good look into my heart for once. Normally, I don't really examine my feelings much. Like you said, I just bottle them up and let them fester. Well, today, they got the better of me. I was after blood. I *wanted* blood. And I *enjoyed* hurting Rory. That's what scares me—what I saw inside myself. The anger, the hatred, the willingness to kill. I saw it all in there, and I don't like it.''

Toni laid a hand on his arm again. ''I think I'm starting to see your problem,'' she said gently. "You always thought that you were in control of yourself, right? That your mind was the one running your body. And now you've discovered that there are all these emotions inside you that won't go away either. And it scares you. But it's not a bad thing, Brandon. We *need* our emotions. You're not Mr. Spock, you're Brandon Mooney. OK, Rory made you aware of your anger, but that's only human. You're not some kind of depraved monster because you lost your cool.''

She almost understood him, Brandon realized, but she couldn't really make the final connection because she didn't know all the facts. "That's not quite it," he told her. "I know I have emotions, and I know they're not all bad. Some of them are actually quite nice. Like enjoying being with you, even if you do make me crazy sometimes. But the other ones, the hatred, the anger, they're so *dark*. Like there's another person living inside me, just waiting to come out.''

"Hey, thanks for the compliment," she said, picking up his comment. He'd hardly been aware he was actually saying that. Any other time, he'd have blushed wildly at the thought, but he was still too depressed. "Look," she continued, "there's a dark side to all of us. I've got one, too. There's a couple of girls I'd like to punch on the nose. But I simply don't give in to those kind of feelings. I channel them away, and refuse to let them take me over. That's all you have to do. Now you've seen the anger, you have to work on making it lose its power over you.''

"It won't work," he told her with terrible certainty. "I can't beat this anger. It's going to overwhelm me.''

"That's just fear talking," she snapped. "You can't possibly know that.''

"Yes, I can," he told her. "That's the entire problem—I *do* know it for a fact."

She stared at him without comprehension. "Would you care to take a whack at explaining that?" she finally asked.

"Remember when I asked you about killing a child that you knew would grow up to be Adolf Hitler?" he asked her.

"Of course. I told you it probably wouldn't make much of a difference."

He nodded. "What if the child who was growing to grow up to become Adolf Hitler was *you*?"

Toni frowned. "Me? You think *I'm* going to grow up like that?"

"No, no," he said hastily. "Not *you—me*."

She stared at him, and then shook her head. "Maybe you were hit on the head too hard," she finally decided. "Brandon, you're a little nuts, but you're nowhere near that bad. You seriously think you're going to grow up to start a world war?"

"Not a war, no," he admitted. "But I know I'm going to grow up to be a killer. That I'll enjoy wrecking the lives of people who've crossed me, or hurt me."

Toni clearly didn't know what to say to this. She attempted to say something twice before thinking better of it. Then she finally made up her mind. "How could you *possibly* know that just from losing your temper with Rory this morning?" she demanded.

"I couldn't, not from just that," he admitted. "But there are other things that you don't know about, and this latest thing just confirms it."

"What other things?" she growled. "Like you've been murdering people and storing them in your basement?"

"No, nothing I've done," he assured her. "It's what I'm *going* to do."

Toni slammed her hand against the tree trunk. "Brandon, you're not making any sense. Start talking. Do you think you've developed psychic powers that enable you to see into the future or something?"

"No," he said. "Not psychic powers. I don't have a clue about that kind of thing. But what I do have, you're not going to believe."

Toni hunched forward and stared into his troubled eyes. He felt a thrill at the contact, but he was still too depressed to even try to understand it. "Try me," she said simply. "If it's scaring you this badly, I'll believe it."

What difference did it make? "You'll think I'm crazy," he told her. "But at this point I don't care. I've met myself— the person I'm going to become. He came back through time and has been speaking to me."

Toni looked worried, and then suddenly thoughtful. "That's who you've been meeting after school these past couple of days?" she asked. "Your future self?"

"That's right." He shrugged. "I know it sounds unbelievable, but he says that I'll invent a time machine in about eighty years, and that's how he came back to meet me."

She chewed at her lower lip for a moment, and then looked up. "Tell me everything that happened," she said.

Brandon did so. He felt a lot better as he told her all about Mooney and what he had said. And what he had done. He kept nothing back, and didn't even care whether she really believed him or not. It just felt good to let it all pour out, and to have her listen to him in stunned silence, even if she didn't believe a word of it. Finally, though, he was done, and he sat there, looking at her.

It was clear that she was having problems with what he'd said. She had to make her mind up whether to believe him or to consider him insane. There wasn't much he could do to help out there, so he just sat and waited. Finally she looked up and sighed.

"That's some story," she said. "And you were right. It's really hard to believe."

"I really didn't expect you to believe me," he admitted. "I'm glad you just listened, anyway. You think I'm crazy, right?"

"You've just talked for fifteen minutes," she snapped. "Now shut up and listen to me for a minute. I said it was really hard to believe, not impossible. Frankly, if anyone else but you had told me that your future self was going to build a time machine, I wouldn't believe them. But you . . ." She shook her head. "If anyone could invent a new super computer that will change the world and then a time machine, it would have to be you. You're almost as smart as you think you are. So, yes, I'm having trouble accepting parts of your story. But I believe you. You're a little wacko, but you're not insane."

He could hardly believe what she had said. "You accept that I'm telling the truth? That I'm not crazy?"

"Yes, I do."

At that moment, the bell rang. Brandon scrambled to his feet automatically, but Toni reached up and grabbed his arm. "We're not finished," she said firmly.

"But . . ." He gestured toward the school. "We're due back."

"Honestly, Brandon," she told him, "I think this is *way* more important than attending classes that neither of us is going to be able to focus on anyway. I wouldn't normally suggest this, but I really think we should cut classes and finish this off once and for all."

Cut classes? Brandon was worried. He'd never deliberately missed a class in his entire life. He knew it was his responsibility to go to school and study. Unlike other people, he'd never really been tempted to skip out on it.

On the other hand, Toni was right. He didn't have a clue what he'd been studying all morning, and there was no way he'd be able to focus on the afternoon classes, either. This business with Mooney was far too disturbing.

"You really think so?" he asked her, hesitating.

"Definitely," she told him. "For one thing, I'm quite eager to meet this Mooney character. I'm tempted to sock him one on the jaw for what he's done to you."

"But he's *me*," Brandon protested.

"He is *not* you," she countered. "He's what you could become, maybe. He's what you'd turn out like if you go bad. But he's not *you* because you aren't like that yet. And, I sincerely pray, you never will be." She jumped to her feet. "Look, we'd better get moving. We can't stay out here because we'll be spotted. Let's head for the woods and see if this maniac is there yet. We have to straighten a few things out with him."

Brandon nodded, and they headed out of sight as quickly as they could. He felt incredibly better knowing that Toni didn't think he was nuts. She believed him, and, perhaps more importantly, believed *in* him. It took a huge weight off his shoulders, and he was starting to feel almost good. Until he remembered Mooney, and knew that this was his fate.

"This Mooney character," Toni said as they walked quickly. "He cheated Rory, and gloated when the idiot offed himself?" Brandon nodded. "And then he wrecked Brianne Waite's marriage and then threw her away because she'd dissed him when he was a kid?" Again, he nodded. "So, what do you think about those actions?"

"I think they're disgusting," he told her honestly. "I mean, I enjoyed bloodying Rory's nose, but if that's all I ever do to him, I can live with it. As for Brianne . . ." He shrugged.

Toni glared at him. "As for Brianne, *what*?" she demanded.

Uh-oh . . . it looked like Toni was getting jealous. Maybe it would be better to pretend that he had absolutely no interest in the blond girl at all. But he simply couldn't bring himself to lie to Toni. Blushing, he admitted, "She's really cute and all. But I could stand living without seeing her again." He swallowed. "But I don't think I'd ever be able to say the same about you."

Her anger evaporated, and she punched him gently on the arm. "That's for lusting after her," she said, but smiled as she did so. "If you didn't think she was cute, I'd have suspected there was something wrong with your metabolism. Only don't mention it *too* often, OK?"

"Promise."

"Anyway, where were we?" Toni gathered her thoughts. "Oh, yeah. Look, you think that what Mooney did was way extreme, right? So you would *never* do those things, would you? So you *won't* grow up to be Mooney. It's that simple."

"I wish it were," he replied, depressed again. "But it's just not that simple. Mooney's *here*, and he *did* do those things.

Therefore, no matter how much I may hate them right now, obviously something is going to happen to me that will make me change my mind. Mooney knows what it is, but I don't have a clue. I'm doomed, Toni. I'm going to become Hitler, and there's nothing that I can do about it.''

"We'll see about that," Toni said grimly. "Is this the woods?''

He looked around, not realizing that they'd already reached his hideout. "Yes," he replied. "It's not far in. Come on." He led the way to the fallen tree. As they approached, he could see that someone was already there. He was dressed in a black jumpsuit, with his back to them, and was bent over his box of tricks. "That's Mooney," he said, dreading meeting his future self again.

At the sound of his voice, Mooney spun around and stared at the two of them. He looked shocked, but nowhere near as shocked as Brandon did.

Mooney had *changed*. His hair was a lot grayer, and his face more wrinkled. He looked as if he'd aged twenty years. And his left eye was no longer normal. It bulged slightly, and Brandon realized that it wasn't real. It was some kind of artificial implant, glowing redly in the shadows of his face . . .

CHAPTER 9

"WHO IS THIS?" Mooney demanded, staring at Toni. "What is she doing here?"

"She's my friend," Brandon answered. "She knows all about you. I needed someone to talk to."

"You shouldn't have told *anyone*!" Mooney cried. "Who knows how this will affect the time lines?"

"Obviously you don't," Toni commented. "You don't know who I am, do you?"

"Didn't I just say that?" Mooney asked.

Turning triumphantly to Brandon, Toni said, "Then this proves he can't be you. You wouldn't forget me in a mere eighty years, would you?"

"I wouldn't think so," Brandon admitted. "But if *he* doesn't know who you are, I *must* have forgotten, for some reason."

"Or else maybe you've changed what *did* happen," Toni suggested. "Maybe *this* Brandon that led to Mooney never paid any attention to me. And now that you have, you've changed the future."

"If I'd changed the future," Brandon pointed out, "then surely he *would* remember you?" He shook his head. "No. I've not changed anything." Then he realized something. "But *he* has. He didn't look like this yesterday. That artificial eye is new."

"Is it?" Toni smiled. "No wonder you hadn't mentioned how ugly he was, then."

"Mind your tongue, girl," Mooney snarled. He whirled to face Brandon. "What are you talking about? I've looked like this since I was thirty-two. You've never seen me any other way."

This didn't make any sense to Brandon at first. And then he realized suddenly what it meant. "You killed him, didn't you? Troy Ryder? You killed him last night?"

"Yes." Mooney made a chopping gesture with his hand. "And the future is worse than before."

Brandon looked at Toni, who clearly didn't yet understand what was happening. Then he looked back at Mooney. "Where did he live? Where did you kill him?"

"In California, where else?" Mooney, too, didn't see the significance of what had happened.

"But your suit can only travel in time," Brandon insisted. "Not in space. You *couldn't* have gone to California."

"What are you talking about?" Mooney demanded. "Of course it travels in space. Space and time are interrelated. You travel through one as simply as through the other."

Brandon suddenly felt very weary. He sank to the ground,

and shook his head. "Mooney, you don't get it, do you? When you change something here in the past, you're altering the future."

"Of course I am," he growled. "That's the whole point of what I'm doing."

"But you haven't thought it through," Brandon exclaimed. "*You're* a part of the future. When you change something here in the past, you change *all* of the future. And that includes yourself. When you first arrived, your time-field generator could only travel in time, not space. When you killed Brandt, that changed. Now you can travel in time *and* space. When you killed Ryder, you changed. Now you have that artificial eye you didn't have before."

Mooney frowned. "Are you sure of that? I can distinctly recall telling you that my suit travels in time and space when I first met you. And I remember having this eye for fifty years."

"Because *your* time line has changed," Toni said, realizing what Brandon was getting at. "*His* hasn't. He remembers what happened; you remember what's changed."

Mooney considered the point for a moment. "I suppose that does make sense," he agreed. "But it also makes no difference. If I remember my life one way and you another, it's irrelevant. What I now know is what happened."

"You still don't get it, do you?" Brandon said, exasperated. "Your actions here and now are affecting *everything* about the future. Killing Ryder hasn't made things better, has it?"

"No," Mooney conceded. "My world is still dead and contaminated."

"And you're planning another killing, I'd guess?" Brandon persisted.

"What else can I do?" Mooney cried. "I have to make a difference! I can't leave matters as they are now."

"You idiot," Brandon told him. "So far, you've been lucky. All you've changed that we know of is that you've got a better time-field generator and a worse eye. The next time you kill someone, who knows what will happen to you? You may even create a future where you never reach the age of ninety-two. Where you die a lot younger. If you keep up what you're doing, you could end up killing yourself!"

That shook Mooney up, as he considered the point. Then he shook his head. "No. You're just trying to get me to stop my crusade. That can't happen. I can't kill myself."

"But if you did?" Brandon asked, refusing to let the point drop. "Then you would never exist to come back to change the past."

Mooney laughed. "And in *that* case," he pointed out triumphantly, "everything would revert to the way it was before. You'd never have met me, since I didn't come back. You'd grow up, become me, and invent the time-field generator. Then you'd come back and meet yourself."

Brandon was shaken by the thought. "Then you mean that this could be part of a never-ending cycle? That we could have been going through the same actions time after time, changing the future and then changing it back, and *never* making a difference?"

Shrugging, Mooney admitted, "It's possible. But if it *was* happening, we'd never know anything about it."

Brandon shook his head wearily. "This time travel business can really screw up a guy's life, can't it?"

"So it would seem," Mooney agreed. "But in any event, I can't and won't give up now. I will complete my mission, or die trying."

Toni had obviously stayed quiet for long enough. "You're a terrorist," she declared. "You've decided that you alone know best what should be done for the human race. And you've decided that no price is too high to pay for whatever you want done. You're willing to kill and keep on killing, aren't you? No matter how many people have to die?"

"Yes," agreed Mooney. "It's for the good of the human race. I have no other option."

"It's *not* for the good of anyone!" Toni cried. "You've admitted that every change you've made has failed. Your plan isn't working, and it won't work. You have to give it up and try something different."

Mooney snorted. "Such as?"

"I don't know!" Toni told him. "Something with less blood in it, maybe! You're obsessed with killing people you feel are guilty as a method of changing the future. And it's not working."

"I think I know why now," Mooney announced. "Brandon helped me to see it. I'm targeting the wrong people. It's not the *industrialists* I should be eliminating. It's the *politicians*. They're the ones who pass the laws that allow my future to exist. So, logically, they're the ones I should kill to change that future. And I will begin that tonight." He gestured at his trunk. "I've checked the Book. The person behind the weakened laws protecting the environment is Senator George Hartley. If I dispose of him, then the laws won't happen. This time it will work, I know it."

"It *won't*," Brandon insisted. "Toni figured it out. If it

isn't Hartley who relaxes the laws, it'll be someone else.''

"Then I'll kill that other person," Mooney stated. "I'll kill as many as it takes to improve the future."

Toni glared at Brandon. "This guy's obsessed with blood, isn't he? And you still think that *you* could turn into *him*?" She nodded at Mooney. "Tell me: whatever happened to Rory Tucker?"

Mooney grinned nastily. "I paid him back for everything he ever did to me. I bought out his company, wiped him out financially. Then, when he was broken and penniless, I killed him."

Brandon was stunned. "That's not what happened!" he exclaimed. "You told me he killed himself!"

"That was the old Mooney," Toni informed him. "This Mooney is even harder and nastier. Just watching Rory self-destruct wasn't enough for him. He had to take a personal hand in it. And I'll bet he did even worse things to Brianne Waite."

Mooney smiled at a memory he cherished. "Brianne paid for rejecting me," he said. "Where she is now, she can't ever say a harsh word to anyone again."

"I don't think I want to know any more than that," Toni interrupted him. "You're disgusting, Mooney. You're talking your *mission* up as something high-minded and in the service of humanity. But it's not really that at all. It's just you, taking warped and sick vengeance on the people you blame for the mess your world is in. You're sick, Mooney. Twisted, bitter and nasty. You've got to realize that what you're doing is wrong."

Mooney shook his head. "You're just trying to stop me," he growled. "You're the one who's sick." He swung his pistol up to cover her. "One squeeze on this trigger, and every nerve in your body will fry at the exact same instant. You'll die in dreadful agony, pain throughout your body." He smiled. "And I won't have to listen to your stupid voice ever again." His finger tightened on the trigger.

Brandon threw himself in front of Toni, shielding her with his own body. "No!" he cried. "You can't hurt her! I won't let you! I'll kill you first!" He steeled himself for the dreadful blast. But Mooney lowered the gun.

"Compassionate idiot," he snarled. "You know very well that I can't kill you. I don't know why that whining girl means anything to you, but so be it. Nothing either of you can say will change my plans." His hand went to his belt. "The future *will* change!" His fingers tapped in a command, and he vanished.

Brandon collapsed, the tension in his body too much for him. "He's gone to kill again," he gasped. "And there's nothing we can do to stop him."

But Toni had something else on her mind. She knelt down in front of him. "You saved my life," she said quietly, shaking. "Mooney was going to kill me. He could have killed you. You risked your life to save mine."

Brandon nodded, still shaking. "I did, didn't I?"

Toni leaned forward and kissed him quickly. "Thank you, Brandon. You're every bit the hero I always knew you could be. Now, *think*. Maybe you might somehow manage to forget me. But could you *ever* be prepared to kill me like that? Or Rory? Or do to Brianne whatever that monster has done to her?"

Brandon felt a chill pass through his soul. "I would hope not. And I understand what you're saying, Toni. But it's still not working. If I couldn't become *that*, then he wouldn't be around. He'd have changed into someone nicer. But he hasn't. And that means that, whether I like it or not, *he's* the monster I'm going to become." He was shaking again, and felt like throwing up. "I hate it," he whispered. "And I hate him. And I hate *me*."

"Stop feeling sorry for yourself," Toni told him firmly. "We've got work to do."

"Work?" Brandon didn't understand her. "What are you talking about? What do we have to do?"

"Stop Mooney, of course," Toni said, as if it were the most obvious and simplest thing in the world.

Brandon staggered to his feet. "But I tried that last night. I tried to warn Ryder. But I failed. The police didn't believe me. And I couldn't warn him directly. I failed yesterday, and I'll fail if I try again."

"Don't be such a defeatist," Toni told him. She grabbed his hand. "Maybe *you* couldn't do anything. But *I* sure can."

Brandon couldn't understand her. "What are you talking about? You'll have no better luck than I did if you try contacting the police. They won't believe you, either."

"Wrong." Toni smiled and shook her head. "You don't know much about me, do you?"

Since that was true, he shook his head. Until she'd approached him two days ago, he'd barely paid any attention to her. Now, though, she'd somehow become very important to him. He could still almost feel the tingle he'd felt from her kiss.

"My mother's the sheriff," Toni explained. "Trust me, *this* time the police will listen to you. Or else Mom's going to have a lot of trouble at home."

Toni was turning out to be quite an amazing girl. However, Brandon wasn't so sure that this would be a good move. "We can't tell them the truth," he objected. "Nobody would believe it. And I was kind of hoping to be able to do this anonymously."

"We'll tell them as much of the truth as they can handle," Toni replied. "And Mom will make sure your name is kept out of this, don't worry. Now, let's go before it's too late."

"One last thing," he told her, gesturing at the trunk. "Mooney keeps some of his equipment in here that we might be able to use."

"It's bound to be locked," Toni pointed out.

"Fingerprint lock," Brandon replied with a grin. "And I have the same prints as Mooney." He bent down and touched the lock. As he had expected, the lid sprang open. He took out the Book and handed it to Toni. He grabbed the Helmet, and then slammed the lid shut. "Now it's time to go."

They hurried to the police station, where Toni greeted the person at the desk and asked for her mother. The policeman gestured toward the back of the building.

"Her office," Toni explained. "Come on." She led the way through the room, rapped on the door marked SHERIFF FROST, and then led the way in.

Brandon followed her, definitely reluctantly. He felt ill at ease here, and wanted to be almost anywhere else. But Toni was right—they had to try to protect Senator Hartley first. Toni's mother glanced up from the folder she was reading at her desk. She looked a lot like Toni, with dark hair down to her shoulders. She frowned at her daughter.

"Aren't you supposed to be in school?" she asked.

"We can't all be where we're supposed to be," Toni answered. "Mom, there's a lunatic who's going to try to assassinate Senator Hartley anytime now."

Sheriff Frost closed the folder and stood up. "You're absolutely sure of that?" she demanded.

"Yes," Toni said. She gestured at Brandon. "This is Brandon Mooney. He and I both heard the man threaten to kill the senator."

Her mother frowned again. "Then we have plenty of time to stop him," she said. "The senator's in the state house, and it will take several hours to get there."

"Several minutes," Brandon said quietly. "He's got methods of travel that you can't even start to understand."

Sheriff Frost's eyes narrowed. "That sounds a tad . . . fantastic."

"I know," he agreed. "But it's true. He could be there now. You've *got* to arrange protection for him. After that, I'll try to explain."

The sheriff stared at him, and then at her daughter. Then she picked up the phone. "Get me the state police," she ordered the operator. "Tell them we've got an emergency on our hands."

Yes! Toni had been correct—her mother was taking action. Maybe this time they could stop Mooney before he killed again.

CHAPTER 10

MOONEY PREFERRED TO work at night, when there was less chance of being seen. However, in this case, he knew that the senator would be in his offices in the capitol building, working alone. That would make it a lot simpler for him to kill his victim than to try to get him alone at home this evening. Hartley had recently remarried, and he and his new wife were virtually inseparable. Mooney couldn't see any way of killing Hartley at home without being forced to kill his wife as well. If he was forced to, he would have done it, but he preferred not to harm any innocents along with the guilty.

And Hartley was as guilty as sin. The Book had made that perfectly clear. In three days, he would propose the bill that would allow greater amounts of insecticides to be used in spraying crops. This would, in the short term, improve the production of crops. But in the long term, the pesticides would wash into the streams and rivers. Fish would ingest them, storing the pollutants in their bodies. Birds, bears and people would eat those fish, and get concentrated doses of pesticides as a result. When any of them reproduced, the pesticides would be further concentrated. They would produce deformities, brain damage and, frequently, simply kill the babies.

In ten years, this part of the country would have a declining birth rate and rapidly disappearing wildlife. Hartley's actions would kill or cripple millions.

And, on top of that, Hartley was actually taking bribes from industry in exchange for his vote or his influence. The man was scum, and Mooney felt absolutely no qualms about killing the man.

The state capitol normally had just a couple of security guards at the door to check arrivals. Mooney frowned when he saw that there were also six police officers, and that they were scanning the people approaching the building, as if they were looking for something.

Him?

Was it possible that Brandon had betrayed him? That, somehow, he had alerted the police, and they had *believed* him? Mooney didn't see how this was possible. Surely his younger self wouldn't betray him? And, even if he tried, why would the police believe him? Then again, it was always possible that Brandon *had* betrayed him. He'd never made any attempt to hide his opinion that Mooney was wrong in his quest. Mooney had naively believed that all Brandon would do was protest. But there was that girl with him . . . Toni Frost. Maybe *she* was the one who had betrayed him? She

was a loudmouthed, opinionated brat, and Mooney could easily believe that she had alerted the police.

If that was so, then he was going to have to fix her. He
concentrated as hard as he could, but there was nobody in his
memory by the name of Toni Frost. If that was so, how could
he possibly have forgotten her?

Then he had an answer. If he, Mooney, were to kill her,
then she'd cease to exist. And perhaps that would make Brandon forget about her, which was why Mooney no longer re-
called her. That made some kind of sense. It also meant that
he had to make her his next priority after this part of the
mission was over.

But for now, he had to get into the building. If he could
see where he was going, and be sure that the way was clear,
he could just jump there using his time-field generator. But
without a line of sight, there was no way to be sure he
wouldn't materialize inside something. And that could be very
unpleasant.

But there was another way out of this problem.

He set the time-field generator to run a second ahead of
current time. To anyone watching, it would look like he'd
vanished, even though he was effectively still there. People
might see something flicker out of the corner of their eyes,
but they wouldn't be able to actually see him directly. He
couldn't shoot the senator in this state, of course, but once he
was in the room with the man, he could drop back to standard
time.

Boldly, he walked up the steps to the capitol building, and
slipped carefully past the guards. He was out of phase with
them in time, but if he bumped into one of them, they'd feel
it a second later. It would probably only puzzle them, but it

was best not to cause problems. As he walked past the policemen, one of them spun around, looking vaguely in his
direction. He must have caught a glimmer of Mooney's pas-
sage, but he could see nothing now. He said something to his
partner which Mooney couldn't catch. Voices sounded very
odd in this state, their temporal shift causing distortion in his
ears.

Mooney glanced down at the sheet of paper the policeman
held. It was a fax of a sketch, and it definitely showed
Mooney's face. That little brat *had* betrayed him! They were
looking for him. Well, he'd fix her as soon as this was over.

He walked down the corridor, again avoiding contact with
anyone or anything. He knew where Hartley's office was from
the Book. As he marched along, he saw several other policemen, including two outside the senator's door. They were all
scanning the corridors, clearly expecting trouble. Thankfully,
they had no real idea what sort of trouble they were about to
have.

Outside the door, Mooney paused. There was no way to
open it without being observed, and he didn't want to have
to wait around until someone else came to open it. That might
take hours, and he couldn't stay in displacement that long.
No, the only thing he could do right now was to take a cal-
culated risk and jump through the door into the room. If he
landed just inside the door, there wasn't much chance of ma-
terializing inside any furniture—it was unlikely that they'd
barricade the door! But there might be another guard there,
and that could be dangerous.

Still, it was a risk he was going to have to take. He set his
belt controls, and then activated the jump.

Now he was standing safely inside the senator's office. He

hadn't materialized inside anyone, thank God! In fact, there was only one person in the room, Hartley himself, working at his desk. He obviously didn't intend to be too disturbed by the security measures being taken to protect him. His one concession had been to close the blinds and move his desk to a wall away from the window.

Naturally, the senator couldn't see him, since Mooney was still in displacement. Mooney drew his pistol, and then flicked the control to return him to temporal stability. Hartley jerked upright as, to his view, a man suddenly appeared out of thin air in front of him. Mooney fired immediately.

The electrical blast from the gun ripped through Hartley's body, setting every single nerve in his body on fire. The senator screamed as he died. Mooney's hands flew over the belt controls, setting them to return him to the woods. As he activated the control, the door flew open and the two armed policemen leaped into the room. One fired, just as Mooney vanished.

For a second, though, Mooney thought that he was dead. He saw the gun come up and then fire. The bullet was a spilt second away from his head when the room vanished and he was standing in the woods again. He almost collapsed in relief, realizing how close he had come to death. And it was all the fault of that whining girl. Well, she didn't have long left to live.

First, though, he had to check on the success of his latest mission. This time he felt a lot more confident that he had succeeded. Brandon had spotted the problem with his original plan. It didn't matter how many industrialist polluters he killed, there would always be more. But by selectively removing corrupt politicians, he could change the world. He crossed to his trunk and opened it.

And stared in disbelief at the gaps in it. The Book and Helmet were both gone. But *how*? Nobody in this primitive time had any way of opening the trunk. It was keyed to open only for him.

And then he understood the full nature of the betrayal. It hadn't been the girl who'd betrayed him, after all. It had been *Brandon*. He had betrayed himself. How could the boy have done such a terrible thing? Surely he had never been such a dreadful person? To betray the future like this!

Well, no matter. Whatever Brandon's reasons were for doing it, it was up to Mooney to fix things. And if that meant fixing Brandon, too . . . well, so be it.

Sheriff Frost had listened to the story that Brandon and Toni had told her with a strained expression on her face. Brandon couldn't see how she could possibly believe them, and felt that even making the attempt was futile. Toni, of course, felt differently, and whatever Toni decided upon was, it seemed, what always got done. When they had finished, the sheriff simply sat there, looking from one to the other of them without any expression on her face. Then she glanced at the Book and the Helmet, both perched on the edge of her desk.

"Frankly," she said finally, "I'm tempted to run every drug and alcohol test we've got on the both of you. And maybe a barrage of psych tests, too." Then she sighed. "But it wouldn't do any good, would it?"

"No," Toni told her. "You know me, Mom. I'm straight. And Brandon's so straight you could use him as a ruler."

"That's what I'm afraid of," the sheriff said with another

deep sigh. "It means that this crazy story has got to be true, and I don't know if I can take that. I'd sooner think you're lying, crazy or high on something. But you're my daughter, and I know you too well for that." She glared at Brandon. "And, from the predatory look in my daughter's eye, I'm likely to get to know you a lot better, too. So, okay." She spread her hands wide. "I believe you both. I've got a time-traveling assassin loose in my town. Now, do you have any idea how we can catch him?"

Brandon gestured at the Book and Helmet. "Bait," he said simply. "Mooney needs those to let him know if what he's done has worked."

Toni nodded. "Smart idea. Then we have to stop him using his belt controls. That's how he time-jumps."

"Oh, well, *that* should be easy," her mother grumbled. "Well, I'll just have to—" She broke off as the phone rang. She scooped it up and answered it. Her face went tense as she did, and then she rang off. "Hartley's dead," she said softly. "It *looks* like natural causes, but one of the guards swears he saw a ghost in the room."

Brandon's hopes were dashed. "Mooney," he said, his voice dulled by pain. "We couldn't stop him after all."

"That's what it sounds like," agreed Sheriff Frost.

Toni stared at Brandon, worried. "He's bound to head back to the woods to check on his progress," she pointed out. "And then he'll know you've betrayed him."

"It should take him some time to figure out where we are, though," Brandon answered. He glanced down at the Book and the Helmet. "Well, let's see what he's done to his world this time." He reached out and pulled on the Helmet.

And this time, all he saw was darkness. There was nothing

there. He removed the Helmet and looked at it, puzzled. "It's not working," he said. "Maybe there's a switch somewhere in this thing that I don't know about?" He examined the Helmet, but saw no sign of any control. "It's supposed to activate when you put it on your head, though."

"Maybe it *is* working," Toni suggested. "Maybe it's showing nothing because there's nothing there to show."

What she was saying made his skin crawl. "You think that this time around Mooney might have somehow destroyed *everything*?"

"Maybe not everything," Toni answered, looking just as sick as he felt. "Just the building where his equipment is. The Helmet's picking up signals from a generator there. If the generator's gone, there's nothing to receive."

Brandon nodded, but he was still puzzled. "Maybe Mooney's managed to kill himself this time?" he suggested. "That way, there wouldn't be any generator."

"If that had happened," Toni argued, "then the Book and Helmet should have vanished, too. And they haven't."

Brandon growled. "I *hate* this time travel stuff," he complained. "So little of it makes sense."

"How do you think I feel?" asked the sheriff. "I'm even more out of it than you are. But what about the Book? If that's a history of the future, maybe that will tell you what's happening there now?"

"Right," Brandon agreed excitedly. "Mooney said that this changes to reflect what's happened once he's changed time." He tapped the keyboard, and the display window at the top of the Book lit up. "OK, let's see what's happening this day in eighty years." He put in the date, and then hit "Enter."

Nothing came up.

"I'll scroll backwards," he said, worried. Was he doing something wrong, after all?

There were no entries for almost five years. And then he found something that chilled him clean through to his bones.

"Atomic war," he gasped, scanning the entry. "Most of the human race has been wiped out. Just pockets are left alive. Obviously, Mooney must have been one of them. They're slowly dying out from radiation poisoning. It happened in the year . . . 2021 . . ." He looked up at Toni and her mother. "President Dundee and the Chinese had a confrontation. Neither one backed down, and they unleashed war. It wrecked the whole world, leading to the almost complete annihilation of the human race. Barely one percent survived, and they were all sterile. Most of them were also infected with radiation poisoning. By 2075, there were less than a hundred people left alive in the entire world. That's the last entry in the Book."

"But Mooney must have been one of the survivors," Toni said, her voice thin and shaking. And he still was able to build his time-field generator."

"The idiot!" Brandon yelled, slamming his fist down on the desk. "The total jackass! He's been trying to stop his world from being polluted, and now look what he's done. He's murdered the entire human race!" He went weak, and almost fainted. "*I've* murdered the human race." He shook his head. "I'm worse than Hitler ever dreamed of being."

"Snap out of it," Toni growled, shaking him. "Mooney *isn't* you. You can't possibly turn into him. It's not possible."

"It doesn't matter now," Brandon answered. "Because Mooney's efforts have made *this* the future. We've got about twenty years left to live, and then the entire human race dies."

Another thought occurred to him. "And I'll live through the blast. Maybe *that's* what turns me into Mooney. Living through the war that I've caused. Mooney's gone insane. It's why he doesn't remember you, Toni. And why he kills people without a problem. He's gone crazy from what he's done."

"It's possible," Sheriff Frost admitted.

"No!" Toni insisted. "It's *not* possible. Brandon, snap out of it! You're not Mooney. You won't ever become Mooney. If *he* can cause the death of the human race, then there's got to be something we can do to avert it."

"There's something that you can do," Brandon agreed, his heart beating swiftly as he suddenly knew the answer to everything. "You can change that future very easily." He looked at Sheriff Frost. "You've got a gun—use it on me. Kill me now. Then I won't be able to grow up to become Mooney. You hear me?" he yelled. "The only way to save the future is to shoot me, now!"

CHAPTER 11

I T TOOK ALL the courage Brandon had to blurt out those words, but he meant every one of them. Things had finally fallen into place for him, and now he understood. For the good of the human race, he had to die. This way, Mooney would never exist, and he would never be able to come back in time and create the havoc he had. Everything would return to normal once again. All he had to do was die.

Then Sheriff Frost shook her head. "No way," she told him. "Aside from the fact that I'm supposed to protect people's lives and not end them, I doubt my daughter would be very happy with me if I killed her boyfriend."

"You don't understand!" he told her desperately. "By killing me, you'll save the world. It's the only thing to do!"

"Then we'll have to figure out some other way of saving

the world," Toni said firmly. "Look, it's really sweet of you to want to be a martyr for the whole human race, but I don't think we need to be quite that extreme."

"It's the only way to stop me from becoming Mooney," Brandon insisted. "If I'm dead, he won't exist."

"Let's just say for a minute that you're right," the sheriff said. She held up a hand to stop Toni's impending outburst. "Let me finish, young lady! Thank you. Let's just suppose that you're right. That the only way to stop Mooney is to kill you. We wouldn't have to do it now. He's eighty years older than you. Anytime in the next eighty years will do the trick."

"No, it won't," Brandon assured her. "You see, if Mooney is left around, he's going to keep on killing people, trying to create his perfect world. And the next time he acts, he may do even more damage. Right now, the world's got about twenty years left to live. What if his next action results in it having twenty *minutes* to live? He's so crazy, who knows what he could do? The only safe, definite way to stop him is to kill me right now."

"Have you got a death wish or something?" Toni demanded. "You don't *know* that's the only solution. It's possible that there's some other way to stop him. And as long as that's a possibility, nobody kills you without killing me first." She folded her arms and glared at him. "I've decided that you're the guy I want, and that's all there is to it."

Her mother gave a chuckle. "She's very stubborn, Brandon. It sounds like you'd better start getting used to it. She sounds like she's planning a long life together."

Brandon would have been touched and pleased any other time to hear that Toni liked him that much. But why couldn't they see what had to be done? "If you won't kill me, I'll have to do it myself,'' he snapped. He lunged across the desk.

Sheriff Frost and Toni both grabbed him and stopped him.

''If you try that again, I'm locking you up,'' the sheriff promised him. ''And I'll take your belt and laces from your sneakers so you can't hang yourself. Nobody commits suicide in my jail. I've a record to protect here.''

''And if you think you can kill yourself,'' Toni added angrily, ''then you'd better be prepared to murder me first. Because I'm not going to let you do it.''

Brandon felt frustrated. Why wouldn't they understand?

And then Mooney was with them. ''Murdering you first sounds like a good idea to me,'' he announced.

All of them gasped in shock when they saw Mooney—not from the threat, but from his appearance. He looked even older now. The artificial eye was gone, but that was the only improvement in his looks. His skin was blotched and gray, and there were sores all over his face, neck and hands. They were red, purple, yellow, and all inflamed. He had virtually no hair, and his left eye was milky white.

''You've got radiation poisoning,'' Brandon gasped, staring at the ailing man in disgust.

''Everyone who survives in my time has it,'' Mooney growled. ''Of course I do. I don't have long to live, but I've the time to fix this.'' He had his weapon out, but it was trained on the sheriff, not Toni. ''I've been listening to your little conversation for quite a while,'' he explained. ''I've heard what happened to get my world into this state. Now I can fix it. But I can't take the chance that the three of you might stop me. So it's time for you all to take a little trip.''

''What are you talking about?'' the sheriff demanded. ''I'm

not going anywhere, and neither is my daughter. Stop this madness now, Mooney.''

Mooney shook his head, coughing as he did so. ''I have to prevent this war,'' he said. ''You can either come with me or I'll kill you here and now. You must know by now what this gun can do.''

It didn't look like it had before. Brandon shook his head. ''That's changed, too,'' he said. ''It doesn't look like any of the previous ones I've seen.''

''Oh.'' Mooney chuckled. ''Well, it fires a concentrated blast of radiation. Enough to fry your brains in half a second. So, take your choice: come with me, or die here.''

''I'll die here,'' Brandon announced, moving toward Mooney.

''Not you, you noble-minded simpleton,'' Mooney snapped. ''These two. You know very well I can't afford to kill you.''

Brandon hadn't really expected him to do so, but he sagged in defeat anyway.

''So, Sheriff,'' Mooney said. ''What's it to be? Do I kill your daughter and you?''

Sheriff Frost sagged. ''No,'' she said quietly. ''You don't. We'll come with you.''

''Smart choice.'' He gestured with his pistol. ''Take off that gun really slowly, and toss it into the corner there.'' As she did as he commanded, Mooney nodded approvingly. ''Good girl. Now, come around to this side of the desk, and join your daughter and my younger self.''

The sheriff moved around, and put a protective arm about her daughter. ''This isn't going to work,'' she said.

''We'll soon find out,'' he told her. ''I have no choice but

to kill this Dundee.'' He nodded to Toni. ''Pick up the Book,''
he ordered. And to Brandon: ''And you get the Helmet. Make
one wrong move and your girlfriend's brain is history.''

He had no option but to obey Mooney. As much as the man
he would become had disgusted him before, it was nothing
compared to how he felt now. ''You're scum,'' he told Mooney.

''I'll have to see about educating you a little after I'm done
here,'' Mooney replied. ''This gun can fire a beam of varying
intensity, and I know a great deal about the brain. A little
skilled work, and you'll come to understand and appreciate
me more.''

Brandon was disgusted and scared. Mooney was aiming to
perform some kind of mental erasure on him, to change the
way he thought. Was *that* how Mooney came into being?
Through altering Brandon's mind?

Now that Mooney had the three of them together in front
of him, he did something to a backpack he was wearing. Brandon hadn't been looking at it before, but he realized what it
had to be. ''That's the time-field generator,'' he said. ''It's
not a small belt anymore. It's a lot bigger.''

''If I'd had the time, I would have made it more compact,''
agreed Mooney. ''I was indeed thinking of a belt version. But
I didn't have the time, or the resources. As you can probably
imagine, most electronic parts were obliterated in the nuclear
war. I had to work with whatever was available. Still, this
works well enough. And you're all close enough.'' He pulled
what looked like a TV remote control from the pack. It was
connected to the pack by thick wires. Using this, he programmed in a destination, and then triggered the device.

There was a weird sinking feeling in Brandon's stomach.

He realized that the time-field generator's abilities had altered once again with the change in the time line. Instead of working only on Mooney, it enveloped the three of them, too—and part of the floor on which they were standing. The sheriff's office vanished, though they were still standing on the floorboards, and they were now in the woods, by the fallen tree.

Sheriff Frost stared around, amazed. "That's incredible," she said. "You've moved us through space instantaneously."

"Not quite," Mooney corrected her. "You're an hour further forward in time, too. It's the shortest time jump I can make with this crude equipment." He gestured with the gun at the trunk. "We need that, too. I'm not leaving it where it can be found again. Just in case. Move over to it, all of you. We've another jump to make."

Since he still had the weapon trained on Toni, Brandon had no choice but to obey. The three of them did as they were instructed, and Mooney moved after them. He programmed in another destination on the handset, and then triggered it.

It was weird seeing the section of floor from the sheriff's office in the woods. It was just as strange when part of the forest floor went with them on the jump.

Brandon had no idea where they were, but they had materialized in some sort of basement, by the look of it. There was a small window high in the wall and an old, abandoned oil heater. Aside from that, there were scattered empty boxes and lots of dust. Wherever this was, obviously it wasn't visited very often.

"When I came to this time," Mooney told them, "I thought having a backup spot would help. This is the basement of the building that used to stand where my house stands in the future. The three of you should be safe here while I work." He gestured with the gun again at Sheriff Frost. "I can see that you have a couple of sets of handcuffs in your jacket pocket. I want you to give me the keys." She did so, wordlessly. "Good. Now, all three of you over to the heater."

Once they were standing beside it, Mooney ordered them to hold out their hands. "Now, Sheriff, I want you to handcuff his right hand to her left, behind the vertical pipe by the wall."

Brandon stood where Mooney indicated, his back to the outer wall. Toni stood on the opposite side of the pipe. Reluctantly, her mother handcuffed them together as she had been ordered. Both of them still had a fair amount of movement possible, but the pipe was only three inches from the wall, so they were effectively trapped.

"Good," Mooney said, coughing again. "Now chain yourself to the other pipe."

Sheriff Frost put one half of the remaining handcuffs on her wrist, and then snapped the other part around a second pipe. She could move along the pipe, but not away from it. "Satisfied?" she asked.

"Perfectly," Mooney answered. He glared at Toni. "I've begun to suspect that you're responsible for the foolish behavior of my younger self. If I'm right, then I'm going to have to kill you to solve the problem. Any interference from you right now, and I'll kill you anyway."

"If you even try to harm her," Brandon told him coldly, "then I'll find some way to kill myself, so you'll die, too."

"That's the only thing keeping her alive right now," Mooney informed him. "I wouldn't have bothered doing this otherwise. Now, I need to find out all about this Dundee. I have to stop an atomic war." He crossed to where Toni had placed the Book on the trunk, and keyed into it. He started to scan the entries, looking for the information he needed.

Toni crept closer to the pipe. "Any chance you can get us out of this?" she asked Brandon.

"Houdini I'm not," he replied. "But we have to do *something*, or he'll kill again. He's obsessed with the idea that he can murder his way to a perfect world."

"He's a typical terrorist," Sheriff Frost said quietly. "Completely convinced that their way is the only possible path, and they stick to it no matter who gets hurt. I don't think we can talk him out of it. Which means that we have to come up with some other solution."

Brandon grunted. "Well, I think any plan that calls for jumping him and overpowering him isn't likely to work, either." He rattled the handcuff against the pipe. "And we don't exactly have a lot of other options."

Mooney put down the Book, and then returned to them. "I've found out what I need," he told them, coughing. There were specks of blood on his lips now. "I'm going to have to act quickly, because I don't have very much longer left to live. Killing Dundee will result in some sort of change. Maybe it won't make my world perfect, but it could hardly affect me worse than this." He indicated his dreadful skin.

"You might wipe yourself out this time," Brandon told him.

"It would still be better than living with radiation poisoning," Mooney told him. "I'll be back shortly." He took the remote control from his pack and worked the controls for a few seconds. Then he vanished.

Brandon crumpled inside. "That's it," he said, his voice tight. "He's gone, and we're stuck here. There's no way we can possibly stop him now."

CHAPTER 12

MOONEY MATERIALIZED CLOSE to Dundee's home. In twenty years, he would be the president of the United States, but right now he was simply a very successful lawyer. His house was large and pleasant, set back from the road, with a gravel driveway leading to the main door. There was a low hedge about the property, and several tall trees dotted the lawn. Flower beds by the house were neatly tended, no doubt by gardeners. It was a pleasant home, and Mooney felt a twinge of nostalgia. It was the kind of house he hadn't seen since the war.

In his own time, the world was gray and dust-filled. Virtually all living things on the Earth had been wiped out. He and the handful of other survivors lived on canned goods, scavenged from the ruins of supermarkets. When they were gone . . . well, it didn't matter. The few people left alive in his world would die before they ran out of food. And then the Earth would be a cold, dead world forever.

Unless he could prevent the war. And there was only one way to do that: to kill the madman who would start it, Dundee. Nothing was going to prevent Mooney from doing that. It was his only hope of saving the world from extinction.

There was no sign of guards. Why should there be? Dundee wasn't yet a public figure, so he really didn't need very much security. Probably just a simple burglar alarm on the house. That certainly wouldn't deter Mooney. He didn't even need to get into the place. He just needed one clear shot at his target, and his world would be safe.

And, hopefully, he would change, too. If his world no longer died in atomic fire, then he would no longer suffer from the radiation poisoning that had affected his entire body and was killing him. He'd be free of it, and better equipped to continue his mission as long as was needed.

It was time to kill . . .

"Don't be such a defeatist!" Toni snapped at Brandon. "There's *got* to be something we can do. We can't just allow him to go on killing people."

"And," her mother added, with a cold edge to her voice, "he's threatened to kill my daughter. If, as I suspect, you have some feelings for her, then you'd better come up with a solution for Mooney very quickly."

Brandon felt utterly helpless and incapable. "It's no good," he protested. "I can't think of any way to stop him. And we're stuck here, chained to these pipes." He glared at the sheriff. "You should have killed me when you had a chance. That would stop him."

"Tempting as the offer to kill you might start sounding," the sheriff replied, "I wouldn't do it. There has to be another option."

Toni grabbed his arm with her free hand. "Brandon, you're the smartest person that I know," she pleaded. "You've got to be able to think your way out of this. There has to be something we can do."

"If there is, it won't come to me," Brandon told her. "It looks like I'm doomed to become Mooney. Much as I now hate what he's doing, obviously something is going to happen to me to turn me into him. I just don't know what it is."

The sheriff slammed her hand down on the old heater, raising a cloud of dust and rust. "For a smart kid," she commented, "you're rather stupid. Maybe *you* don't know what it is, but *that* does." She pointed at the Book, lying on the trunk where Mooney had dropped it.

A flare of hope was born inside Brandon as he stared at it. "Of course!" he exclaimed. "If that's a history of the future, then what happens to me must be in its record." Then the reality of their situation sunk in. "But it's no good. The Book's over there, and we're trapped here."

"So there might well be some way out of this that doesn't include killing you?" asked the sheriff. She seemed awfully cheerful, for some reason.

"Of course," he agreed. "If I can discover what it is that turns me into Mooney, then we can change it. That should solve everything. But we can't get at the Book. We're stuck here."

"No, we aren't." Sheriff Frost fished a pair of keys from the pocket of her jeans. "Do you think I'm stupid enough not to carry spare keys for my handcuffs?'' She proceeded to unlock herself.

Brandon stared at her in astonishment. ''You mean that you could have freed us at any time?''

''Sure.'' She set about unlocking his cuffs. ''But I wasn't going to set you free if you were going to kill yourself.'' Then she grinned. ''Besides, I thought the two of you might enjoy being chained together.''

''Mom!'' Toni exclaimed, shocked and a little amused. ''We haven't even been on a *date* yet.''

Brandon tried to ignore their baiting of one another. He dashed across the basement, and seized the Book. Quickly, he typed in his own name and the ''Search'' function. Information began to form on the screen.

It was really weird, sitting there and reading about what he was going to do:graduate . . . go to Harvard . . . scholarships . . . first job . . .

The answer was in here somewhere. It *had* to be. It was just a matter of finding it.

And praying that he was in time to save Dundee's life.

Mooney crouched in the back garden, staring in through the slightly open French windows of the house. Dundee was inside, with his family. He and his wife and a young girl, about eight years old. They were having afternoon tea, by the look of it. It seemed an almost idyllic picture. All three of them seemed to be very happy.

Tough. The fact that Dundee was a nice family man didn't mean anything when weighed against the future. He had to die, so that the Earth could live. It was that simple.

Another spasm racked Mooney's body. This time, there was

a sharp pain inside his chest. He fought for his breath as his whole body cavity seemed to burn in agony. Finally, he managed a long, cough-filled breath.

He was running out of time. His heart was giving out. His body shook with pain and weakness, and he knew that he didn't even have the strength left to walk to the open window and shoot down Dundee. He would die as he tried it.

But there was another way to finish him, one that he could manage. He adjusted the spread of the radiation pistol, setting it on high-intensity overload. Immediately, the power began to build up, producing a slight whine. In about ten seconds, the power couplings would short out, and the weapon would turn into a small but very deadly grenade. It would explode, killing everything within the room.

That would include Mrs. Dundee and their cheerful daughter. Mooney didn't want to do it, but he had no choice. In every war, there are innocent casualties. They were just two people in the wrong place at the wrong time. They would die so that his own world would live.

With all his remaining strength, Mooney hurtled the gun from his hand, through the open French windows.

Five seconds to go . . .

"Can't you just resolve not to become Mooney?" asked Toni, frantically. "Isn't that enough?"

"No," Brandon answered. "If it was, he'd have gone already. I *hate* everything he believed in. So there's got to be something else. Something that I'll do that leads me to become him."

Then he read the page again, and almost felt like exploding. This was it!

"It's the computer!" he exclaimed, hope and awe surging through him. "It's when I invent this super computer he told me about in seven years. There's some kind of lab accident when I do it that puts me into the hospital for a week. *That's* it! I must have suffered some kind of brain damage."

"You've got to be right," Toni said, her face alive with joy. "So, now what? How do you stop Mooney?"

"Easy." Brandon laughed, and tossed the Book onto the chest. "I won't go into computing. I'll become a marine biologist or something instead. That's all. I *won't* invent any computer."

As he said this, the trunk and Book vanished.

Dundee looked up from the table as the French windows rattled. Someone had thrown something through them, and . . .

Puzzled, he saw that there was nothing there. He could have sworn he'd seen something come in, but there was nothing there.

Oh, well . . . it must just have been the wind. There was nothing wrong. Nothing at all. "So," he continued, "I had a call today from Jim White. The Democrat. Seems they want someone to run for senator, and my name came up. What do you think about that?"

"It's gone," Sheriff Frost said, staring at the empty spot on the floor. "Brandon, do you think *he's* gone, too?"

"Yes," Brandon said, with absolute confidence. "He's gone. And everything he came back in time to change has gone, too." He grinned at Toni. "I think we'll find that Troy Ryder and Henry Brandt are still alive, too. Since I never became Mooney, he never came back to kill them."

"That's a relief," Toni said happily. Then a sudden thought struck her. "But what about the future? Will it still be terribly polluted?"

"I rather think that's up to you," her mother replied. "And the rest of your generation. You know it's a possibility, but then there's a chance that you can change it. If you make your minds up that it's got to be done." She smiled at them both. "And, frankly, if the two of you can't save the world—again!—then I don't think anybody could."

"We'll do it," Brandon vowed. "Since I'm not going into computing, I can go into something that will be against pollution. I know we'll make the future a better place than it has been."

Toni grabbed his hand. "And I'll help," she promised. "Like Mom said, I'm too stubborn to change, and I've decided that you're going to be mine, whether you like it or not."

"I'm sure I'll like it," he answered, feeling happy and at peace with himself. It was something he'd never really felt before. The anger was gone, and the resentment. And the overwhelming egotism, too. All he'd ever really needed was to be loved and love back. And now, thanks to Toni, he knew he had real stability in his life. He'd never let it go. He felt really lucky that, for whatever reasons she had, Toni had decided to become a part of his life.

It had made all the difference in the world.

Eighty years in the future, Brandon Mooney looked up from his studies as his wife materialized in the laboratory they both shared. His side of the lab was filled with his marine biology work, and hers with her electronics. He was working hard on his cetacean research. He was certain that they'd now reached the point where the whales were strong enough to save themselves. It was the culmination of over seventy years of work. Any threat of pollution destroying the Earth was now over, hopefully forever. Now they were rebuilding the wrecked natural kingdom. The latest medical breakthroughs had suggested that they could live for another maybe two hundred years before they really started to get old. He had plenty of work to keep him busy for that length of time.

His wife smiled at him as she powered down her time-field generator and stepped off the dais. "It worked," she informed him. "I went back eighty years and met myself."

Brandon smiled at her. She still looked lovely, thanks to the nanotech doctors in her bloodstream that kept her in optimal health. "She was a cute little thing, wasn't she?" he asked.

"Wasn't *I*?" Toni replied with a mock frown. "You mean I'm not anymore?"

"You're *always* lovely," he assured her, kissing her nose. "And brilliant. But I always knew you'd make that time generator work. So what did you and your younger self have to talk about?"

"What else?" she asked with a cheeky grin. "*Boys*. I was obsessed with finding a boyfriend back then. So I told her all about you. It seems that she didn't know you, and hadn't ever thought about you until I told her what a wonderful life we've had together. *That* made her decide that you were going to be her choice, come hell or high water."

Brandon laughed. "Yes, I remember that you were very set on marrying me, even when we were quite young. Though I don't quite remember why we first started dating."

"Nor do I, after all this time," Toni admitted. "I rather suspect that my going back in time changed something somehow. I think that I'd better put this belt away under lock and key while I consider its implications. After all, it wouldn't do to go around changing the past, would it?"

"No," Brandon agreed. "It wouldn't. After all, I like the past just the way it is. And the present just as much." He gave her a gentle kiss. "I wouldn't want to change a thing."

EPILOGUE

SOMETIMES THE BEST of intentions aren't good enough. Sometimes they are. And sometimes . . . well, times change, and people change. For us, the future arrives as it always has, one day at a time.

But if you had the power to change something in the past, what would you choose?

Or would you choose to change nothing at all?

THIS STORY IS OVER.

BUT YOUR JOURNEY INTO

THE OUTER LIMITS™

HAS ONLY BEGUN.....

Watch out for The Outer Limits™ series... landing at a bookstore near you soon!

TOR BOOKS

Check out these titles from Award-Winning Young Adult Author
NEAL SHUSTERMAN

Enter a world where reality takes a U-turn...

MindQuakes: Stories to Shatter Your Brain

"A promising kickoff to the series. Shusterman's mastery of suspense and satirical wit make the ludicrous fathomable and entice readers into suspending their disbelief. He repeatedly interjects plausible and even poignant moments into otherwise bizzare scenarios...[T]his all-too-brief anthology will snare even the most reluctant readers."—*Publishers Weekly*

MindStorms: Stories to Blow Your Mind

MindTwisters: Stories that Play with Your Head

And don't miss these exciting stories from Neal Shusterman:

Scorpion Shards

"A spellbinder."—*Publishers Weekly*

"Readers [will] wish for a sequel to tell more about these interesting and unusual characters."—*School Library Journal*

The Eyes of Kid Midas

"Hypnotically readable!"—*School Library Journal*

Dissidents

"An Involving read."—*Booklist*

Call toll-free 1-800-288-2131 to use your major credit card or clip and mail this form below to order by mail

- ✂

Send to: Publishers Book and Audio Mailing Service
PO Box 120159, Staten Island, NY 10312-0004

❑ 55197-4 **MindQuakes** ....$3.99/$4.99 CAN	❑ 52465-9 **Scorpion Shards**............$3.99/$4.99 CAN
❑ 55198-2 **MindStorms** ....$3.99/$4.99 CAN	❑ 53460-3 **The Eyes of Kid Midas** ...$3.99/$4.99 CAN
❑ 55199-0 **MindTwisters**..................$3.99/$4.99 CAN	❑ 53461-1 **Dissidents** ....$3.99/$4.99 CAN

Please send me the following books checked above. I am enclosing $_____. (Please add $1.50 for the first book, and 50¢ for each additional book to cover postage and handling. Send check or money order only—no CODs).

Name _____

Address _____ City _____ State _____ Zip_____

TOR BOOKS

"A GREAT NEW TALENT. HE BLOWS MY MIND IN A FUN WAY."
—Christopher Pike

Welcome to the PsychoZone.

Where is it? Don't bother looking for it on a map. It's not a place, but a state of mind—a twisted corridor in the brain where reality and imagination collide.

But hold on tight. Once inside the PsychoZone there's no slowing down...and no turning back.

The PsychoZone series by David Lubar

❑ **Kidzilla & Other Tales**
0-812-55880-4 $4.99/$6.50 CAN

❑ **The Witch's Monkey & Other Tales**
0-812-55881-2 $3.99/$4.99 CAN

Call toll-free 1-800-288-2131 to use your major credit card or clip and send this form to order by mail

Send to: Publishers Book and Audio Mailing Service
PO Box 120159, Staten Island, NY 10312-0004

Please send me the books checked above. I am enclosing $_____.
(Please add $1.50 for the first book, and 50¢ for each additional book to cover postage and handling. Send check or money order only—no CODs).

Name_____

Address _____

City _____ State _____ Zip _____

DATE DUE

Demco, Inc. 38-293